"Nena," he whispered. "Let me love you—let me be your husband."

"I—I can't…" she responded hoarsely, only too conscious of his scent, of the maleness of him, of everything about him that drew her, while she tried desperately to remind herself of all the reasons she couldn't let it happen.

"I promise not to hurt you," he said reasonably, leaning his hands on each side of her on the balustrade, his tanned face and sensual lips only inches from hers.

She realized with a tingling shudder that left her weak, that he was about to kiss her.

Scottish author FIONA HOOD-STEWART has led a cosmopolitan life from the day she was born. Schooled in Europe and fluent in seven languages, she draws on her own experiences in the world of old money, big business and the international jet set for inspiration in creating her books. She now lives in Switzerland with her two teenage sons.

You can visit Fiona's Web site at www.fionahood-stewart.com.

Fiona is also one of the international collection of bestselling authors writing for MIRA® Books. Her latest novel, *Southern Belle,* is available next month. Look out for a tempting extract at the end of this book.

Her other titles include:

The Stolen Years
"A feast for anyone who yearns for a long, rich read."
—*Romantic Times*

The Journey Home
"Well told…with plot twist and powerful emotions."
—*Romantic Times*

There'll be another great story by Fiona in Harlequin Presents available later this year!

The Brazilian Tycoon's Mistress
is on sale in October, #2432

Fiona Hood-Stewart

THE SOCIETY BRIDE

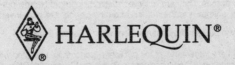

HARLEQUIN®

TORONTO • NEW YORK • LONDON
AMSTERDAM • PARIS • SYDNEY • HAMBURG
STOCKHOLM • ATHENS • TOKYO • MILAN • MADRID
PRAGUE • WARSAW • BUDAPEST • AUCKLAND

ISBN 0-373-12388-4

THE SOCIETY BRIDE

First North American Publication 2004.

This edition published by arrangement with Harlequin Books S.A.

® and TM are trademarks of the publisher. Trademarks indicated with
® are registered in the United States Patent and Trademark Office, the
Canadian Trade Marks Office and in other countries.

Visit us at www.eHarlequin.com

Printed in U.S.A.

CHAPTER ONE

HE'D been summoned, Ramon Villalba realised. He frowned as he sat astride his fine Passo Fino and stared across the wide, green open spaces where several thousand heads of cattle—all belonging to him—grazed, oblivious of the fact that their owner was once again about to board his company jet in Buenos Aires and head for London.

It was rare these days that his father summoned him. After all, Ramon was thirty-two, and had cut his eye-teeth a long while ago. So the matter must be extremely important and the summons immediately met.

He experienced a moment's concern. Could it be the health of one of his parents' that was the issue here? Surely not. His mother, with whom he had an exceptionally close relationship, would have confided in him. Still, he wasted no time in galloping back to the gracious *hacienda,* its ancient terracotta walls bathed in late-afternoon sunlight, and having Juanito, his manservant, pack his bags in readiness for the journey.

Twenty-four hours later he was sitting in the book-lined study of his family's home in Eaton Square, trying to absorb the impact of what his father had just said.

'But that's utterly preposterous!' Ramon exclaimed, dragging his fingers through his thick black hair and shaking his head. 'As I recollect, Nena Carvajal is not twenty yet—a mere girl. How can you and old Don Rodrigo even contemplate marriage for her?'

'Really, Ramon. Stop being prissy. You sound as if you've never heard of a marriage of convenience.'

'Well, certainly not one like this,' Ramon countered with feeling, letting his long legs stretch before him and crossing his ankles. His bronzed brow creased. 'I don't know what's got into your heads. If Nena thinks of me as anything at all it's probably in the light of an—'

'Rubbish.' His father, a well-dressed man in his late seventies, cut him short briskly. 'I doubt if she remembers you at all—which may be for the best.'

'Wonderful.'

'There is a very strong reason for this arrangement.'

'Oh? And what might that be?' Ramon raised a haughty brow.

'Simply put, Don Rodrigo, her grandfather, is dying.'

Ramon frowned and sat up straighter. 'What's wrong with him?'

'The big C, I'm afraid. He has six months at the most. Now, can you imagine what might happen to that girl if she's let loose on the world with the kind of money she will inherit? Not to mention the running of Rodrigo's empire,' he added, with a quick, sharp look at his son.

'So that's what this is all about,' Ramon said slowly. 'Rodrigo thinks I might be a suitable candidate to take over, does he?'

'I would say that is a great compliment, considering the vastness and complexity of his empire.'

'I suppose that's one way of looking at it,' Ramon conceded irritably. 'There's only one problem.'

'Oh?' Don Pedro raised an eyebrow and waited.

'I have no desire to be married.'

A moment's silence followed before the older man answered. 'Ramon, this marriage to Nena—'

'Who could practically be my daughter,' Ramon dismissed disparagingly.

'Hardly. Unless you plan to enter the *Guinness Book of Records* as a very young father,' his parent murmured with a touch of wry humour. 'Now, this marriage—as I was saying before you so rudely interrupted me—will hardly curtail your er—lifestyle. I'm sure that Nena has been brought up to expect a marriage of this kind. I haven't, I admit, seen her for several years. She has been at boarding school—the Convent of the Sacré Coeur,' he continued with a small satisfied smile. 'That in itself is a good omen.'

'Father, this whole notion is totally absurd!' Ramon exploded. He jumped up from the chair, his lean, athletic figure clad in an exquisitely cut Italian navy silk suit, and began pacing the study. 'You'd think it was the Middle Ages. I cannot agree to such a plan.'

'At least give it some thought—think about it,' Don Pedro said reasonably. 'It would, of course, be an incredible opportunity for you. Businesswise, I mean.'

Ramon's eyes flashed and he drew himself up taller. 'If you think, Father, that I would get myself tangled up in a marriage of convenience out of a desire to improve my already not so shabby business ventures, then let me relieve you of the notion immediately,' he replied witheringly.

'I didn't mean it like that,' Don Pedro responded carefully, measuring his son's reaction. 'Think of your mother and I. We barely knew one another before our marriage. And look how wonderfully it has turned out. The truth is I have never looked at another woman since, and I can assure you I was quite a lad in my day.' He let out a long, low laugh. 'And as for age—why, your mother's twenty years my junior. You are barely thirteen years older than Nena. I cannot take that as a consideration. And besides, at thirty-two it is time you thought of setting up your nursery.'

'Whatever, Father,' Ramon growled, suddenly needing to be alone, to think, to straighten this mess out.

'May I tell my old friend Don Rodrigo that you will at least think about the proposal? To turn it down out of hand would be nothing short of an insult.'

This last was true. The honour of being selected by one of the richest men in the world to be his future grandson-in-law, heir to all his responsibilities, was no light matter. Handled wrongly, this could affect a lifelong friendship.

Reluctantly Ramon nodded. 'Very well, Father. But on one condition,' he declared, his chin jutting firmly, 'that I get to see Nena. I presume she has been made aware of the circumstances?'

'Uh, not that I'm aware of,' Don Pedro murmured, carefully shuffling a pile of papers on his desk. 'All in good time.'

'Great,' Ramon replied cynically, rolling his eyes. Then, for some inexplicable reason, he avoided delivering the rest of the sentence about to escape his lips.

*   *   *

'The Villalbas?' Nena's well-shaped brows creased and she tilted her lovely, lightly tanned face to one side, her flashing green eyes fixed on her grandfather. 'I don't seem to remember them. Did we know them back in Argentina?'

'Of course, my love. But it has been quite a while since they last visited. Certainly not since you went off to school. Pedro Villalba is an old and trusted friend of mine, and his wife Augusta is in some way related to your late grandmother's family.'

'Ah.' Nena nodded and smiled. Everyone was always somehow related to the family.

'They are coming to tea tomorrow with their son, Ramon, whom you may remember. He came over once or twice when he was at Eton and then Oxford.'

'Sorry, I haven't a clue who he is.' She shook her tawny gold-flecked hair, highlighted by two weeks of playing tennis every day in the South of France, and jumped up. 'I'm off to the tournament now. Do you need anything before I go? Water for your pills?' she asked, suddenly concerned.

Her grandfather seemed to have aged much during the past weeks, and she worried about him. Not for nothing had she inherited her deceased French mother's perception and innate capability for running Thurston Manor, their lovely country house near Windsor, and for making sure that her beloved grandfather was cosseted.

'No, no, my child. Off you run. Just make sure to be back on time for tea tomorrow.'

'I'll try. But we have the semi-finals, and if I get through today I may be playing.'

Don Rodrigo smiled at her benignly. He loved her so dearly, and wished—oh, how he wished—that he could live to see her bloom into the flower he perceived emerging, watch as she travelled towards womanhood. But that was not to be, he reminded himself with an inner sigh, accepting the soft kiss on his withered old cheek. And he must make sure she was safely provided for. Not just financially—there she was only too well provided for. If anything that was half the worry. In fact what truly concerned him were the fortune-hunters that he knew would hover like anxious vultures from here to Tierra del Fuego the minute he was dead and buried.

It was four by the time the Bentley drew up on the gravel drive before the splendid country house. Ramon experienced another wave of distaste. The whole thing was utterly absurd, and left him feeling as though he were participating in a very bad B movie. Still, he'd listened to his mother's urgings and his father's request to at least honour the visit. And he would, he supposed, alighting from the vehicle. At least after this he might be able to bring his father and Don Rodrigo to reason.

Several minutes later they were being conducted by the dignified white-haired butler onto the lawn, where Don Rodrigo heaved himself with some difficulty out of a wicker chair.

'*Amigos,*' he said, embracing Pedro and kissing Augusta. 'What a pleasure it is to receive you in my home.' Then he turned towards Ramon and eyed him closely. 'How do you do, Ramon? It is several years since we last met, but I've followed your may I say rather brilliant progress?' He quirked a brow and smiled. 'Knowing your father, I am not surprised. But impressed. Very impressed.'

'Coming from you, that is a compliment indeed,' Ramon murmured, shaking the other man's hand. He sensed the slight shaking and frailty in the fingers and realised that the sharp grey eyes belied failing health. He also realised that Don Pedro would not easily be fobbed off. As he sat down next to his mother at the table, already laid for afternoon tea, he wondered just how hard it was going to be to get out of this marriage. There was no sign of Nena, he observed a sudden spark of hope flashing. Perhaps she'd been told and had refused to agree to the arrangement. She was, after all, nearly twenty.

If so, all the better.

He was quite willing to help her out, advise her financially—even be a trustee, if Don Rodrigo so wished.

The thought began to take shape. Perhaps that was the way to work the situation, he mused, his quick brain already solving the matter. If Nena didn't agree to the marriage then he could bow out gracefully and not be blamed, and it would all work out for the best. It was, he reflected, allowing wishful thinking to take the upper hand, a mere question of initiating the correct strategy.

'Have they arrived?' Nena asked breathlessly as she jumped out of her new Audi TT. After throwing her tennis racket onto one of the hall chairs, she glanced at herself in the gilt mirror. 'I look a mess. But I suppose I'd better dash out and say hello, or Grandfather will kill me,' she exclaimed to Worthing, the butler, who was eyeing her severely as he closed the door.

'Don Rodrigo and the guests are on the lawn, Miss Nena.' He still called her by her childhood name.

'Good. Well, do see that tea is served, won't you? Oh, and Worthing? Please ask Cook to serve both China and Ceylon. I don't know which the guests would prefer.'

'Of course, Miss Nena,' he replied, pursing his lips and shaking his head fondly as she flew across the hall, through the drawing room, and down the steps to the lawn, where the group was seated under the chestnut tree facing the lake.

Smoothing her hair back, she hurried across the grass. How nice for her grandfather to have some people to entertain. He saw so few nowadays. She was sure it wasn't good for him to lead such a solitary existence, she reflected as she drew up on them from behind, but perhaps a lot of social activity might tire him.

'Hello, I'm so sorry I'm late.'

Ramon turned.

'Aunt Augusta, Uncle Rodrigo, it's been ages,' she said, kissing Ramon's parents while he looked in frank admiration at the gorgeous, lithe young woman—at her never-ending long bronzed legs that eradicated for ever the fuzzy image he'd formed of a rather dowdy, plump adolescent. Her smile, he reflected, was dazzling, her teeth white and perfect, and her lightly tanned skin set off the beauty of her huge almond-shaped green eyes in a manner fit to leave even a seasoned womaniser like himself dazed.

And her hair…

It fell in feathery wisps from a ponytail, giving her the air of having tumbled straight out of bed, and leaving him in dire danger of an embarrassing physical reaction.

Pulling himself together, Ramon rose and shook hands, hoping none of these untoward emotions showed, and reminded himself of the true nature of their visit here.

'Will you excuse me if I pop upstairs and change?' she was saying to his mother in a charmingly assured manner that belied her youth. 'I look a dreadful fright.'

He watched as she retreated swiftly across the lawn, trying to suppress the delightful image of that long, curved, slim body uncoiling amongst bedsheets, finding himself distressingly prey to a sensual twisting tug. He must not, he realised, removing his eyes from her, lose track of reality here. He caught his father's approving eye and quickly concentrated once more on the conversation.

But if his father thought that Nena's astonishing beauty and charm might make the marriage any more acceptable he was wrong. Instead it somehow made it worse. It was one thing to do a poor dowdy creature a favour, another to place under his protection a paragon whom, when she found her feet, would be the toast of society in every city they visited. The thought was strangely disturbing and he banished it.

'Ramon, I hope you have thought about your father's and my proposition,' Don Rodrigo said, easing himself with obvious difficulty in the wicker chair, reminding Ramon of just how much was at stake here. 'After one look at my lovely granddaughter I'm sure you are aware how impossible it would be for me to allow her to go out alone and unchaperoned into the world.'

'Well, I don't altogether agree, no,' Ramon countered. 'After all, sir, we are in the twenty-first century. A well-selected board of trustees could easily take care of her affairs. She seems a confident young woman, quite able to look after herself,' he added.

'Ha!' Don Rodrigo let out a harsh exclamation. 'Much you know about it. Oh, she's got confidence and charm and excellent manners, of course. But she would be swept off her feet by the first fortune-hunter that walked into her life. And, believe me, they're already lining up,' he said darkly.

'That I can believe,' Pedro Villalba replied, sending his son a meaningful look from under his thick silver brows.

'And it's not only my little Nena I'm concerned about,' Don Pedro continued, meeting Ramon's eyes with a look as steady as his own. 'It's the future of all I've built up over a lifetime. I have no intention for that to go to rack and ruin, frittered away by some spendthrift. Trustees, as you mentioned earlier, are all fine and dandy, but they will not direct her sentimental life, look after her as a woman needs looking after.'

'Excuse me for being so bold,' Ramon said, leaning forward, 'but does Nena have any idea of what's going on here?'

'Up until now I deemed it preferable to stay silent. After all, I do not want her to be unduly upset. And when she learns of my illness,' he said stifling a sigh, 'she *will* be most upset.'

'Of course.' Ramon looked down. 'Don Rodrigo, although I would be more than willing to accept a role in an advisory capacity, I don't feel that—'

'One moment, young man. I am aware that all this

has been thrust upon you in a most impromptu manner. But will you not at least take the opportunity, now that you have come all this way, of getting to know my granddaughter a little better? I am not suggesting that the two of you fall in love, or anything of that nature, merely that together you establish a well-balanced relationship. Nena has been brought up in the strictest possible manner. She would make you a good wife.

'Many marriages work out very well under these conditions,' he added with a thin, tired smile. 'I know that in this day and age you young people all believe in Hollywood-style relationships—marriage one day, divorce the next. But real life, my boy, is very different. Look rather at your parents, and at myself. Our marriages were planned, and they worked out brilliantly.'

'That's all very well,' Ramon countered, but then, seeing the butler carrying a large silver tray piled with scones and sandwiches, he closed his mouth.

Nena rushed into the large marble bathroom of her suite of rooms and took a rapid shower, her mind filled with the incredibly good-looking son of her grandfather's friends. She had been quite taken aback, but hoped that her surprise had not been in any way evident.

He was older, of course, and rather forbidding and arrogant-looking, with his thick black hair, straight Roman nose, high slashed cheekbones and chestnut golden-flecked eyes. A bit like an actor, she reflected, rubbing herself with a thick terry towel before stepping into the dressing room and choosing a short pink linen Gucci dress.

Minutes later she tripped down the stairs and joined the others. She sat in the only available chair, next to Ramon, determined not to let his intense masculine aura distract her as she proceeded to serve the tea. The next few minutes were occupied with handing round sandwiches, and it was only when she sat back down that she realised Ramon was looking at her rather fiercely.

She shifted uncomfortably and suppressed a desire to pull her skirt lower. A delicious shiver coursed through her. She'd heard of men looking at you and leaving you feeling undressed. Now she knew what it meant. For a moment she wondered if she was dreaming. Perhaps she'd spilled something on her dress and that was why he was looking her over in that confident manner.

She glanced down, but there was nothing, and she felt cross with herself for allowing this man to leave her feeling both self-conscious and—something else that she couldn't quite define. Shifting closer to his mother, she half turned her back on him and chit-chatted about this and that for a while, trying not to be aware of his eyes upon her.

'You must come and see the garden properly,' she said to Augusta. 'I've had some new flowerbeds laid out near the lake, and the little wood over there is charming to walk in.'

'Thank you, my love,' Augusta replied with a gracious smile. 'But I'm afraid I find walking a bit of a strain these days, particularly in the heat. But Ramon, I'm sure, would be delighted to see the garden.'

'Oh, no. I don't think you'd like it at all,' Nena said hastily, turning towards him, embarrassed and biting her lip while hoping she hadn't sounded too rude. She could hardly refuse to take him, but the last place she wanted to go was for a walk in his austere, rather autocratic company.

'Yes, Nena, that's a good idea,' her grandfather insisted. 'You take Ramon for a walk while we old folks chat.' Don Rodrigo smiled approvingly.

Unwilling to distress her grandfather by refusing, Nena turned and glanced at Ramon. 'If you like we can go,' she said, her tone unenthusiastic, hoping he'd refuse.

'Fine. Let's go.'

Reluctantly she rose and began walking down towards the lake with Ramon close by her side. He was tall, she observed, at least six foot two or more, and his shoulders were broad. There was something powerful and engulfing in his presence, she realised, an authority about him that reminded her in a way of her grandfather. Now, as they walked, he slipped off his jacket and threw it casually over his shoulder while Nena wondered what on earth to say to him.

Soon they'd reached the lakeside, and Ramon still hadn't made any effort at conversation—although Nena could feel his eyes boring into her. It was really most uncomfortable, especially since he was so close to her. She was catching whiffs of his musky aftershave—and something else indefinable, something she'd never experienced next to any man before.

'Those are peonies and delphiniums,' she blabbered, pointing out the flowers, 'and over there are a number of dahlias. But I'm sure you're not really interested in flowers,' she added quickly, pressing her hands together and wondering why she felt so wound up and nervous when usually she was perfectly at ease with visitors.

'You're right,' he replied, his face breaking into a sudden charming smile that lit up his face as he looked down at her. 'I'm no expert on flowers. But my parents and your grandfather seemed pretty determined that we should come for a walk together, don't you think?' he asked, testing the terrain.

'Yes.' She frowned, looking up at him, puzzled. 'They did, didn't they? Do you have any idea why?'

Ramon wished he'd kept his mouth shut. For now he felt like a cad, as though he was deceiving this young woman by not telling her the truth. Yet how could he come clean when she had not the slightest idea that her grandfather was dying?

'I suppose they thought that we are nearer in age and might find more to talk about on our own,' he said with a non-committal shrug. He found it hard to resist her enquiring gaze, that lovely frank innocence in her eyes and in her charming smile, and the underlying trace of sensuality that he'd be willing to bet she still hadn't recognised in herself. The thought left him in dire danger of another embarrassing physical reaction and he turned quickly towards the lake. 'Look, why don't we keep them happy and you show me this famous wood?' he said, pointing to his left with forced interest.

'Okay,' she agreed, glad that the atmosphere had lightened up. Perhaps he was just someone you needed to get to know better.

'Tell me about yourself,' he said, taking her arm lightly as they reached a small bridge that crossed the lake to a path that led to the wood.

Another curious new sensation coursed through Nena at his touch on her flesh, and she was hard put to it not to shudder.

'There's not much to tell,' she said, allowing him to guide her across, although she knew the bridge by heart. 'I finished school last year. I wanted to go to university—was accepted by a couple, in fact,' she added hastily. For some reason she didn't want him to assume she was stupid. 'But then Grandfather seemed increasingly unwell and I didn't feel I could abandon him.' She stopped and shrugged, then smiled up at him through long thick lashes. 'He doesn't seem any better lately, and I don't want to make him unhappy.'

'But of course you must go to university,' Ramon replied. Part of him was shocked that her future might be compromised. The other part, the part that didn't want to recognise just how attractive he found her, thought how appealing it was that in this day and age, when most women he came across thought only of their own wellbeing and personal ambition, she should place her grandfather first. Which, in turn, reminded him of all the pain she was going to experience when she learned of his terminal illness.

'Maybe one day I'll be able to go to college,' she replied with a shrug. 'I'd really like to. But please,' she said, her brows creasing suddenly, 'promise you won't tell Grandfather? I would hate for him to be upset or worried.'

'Of course I won't say anything. Anyway, it's none of my business. Still, it seems odd that he won't—' Suddenly Ramon remembered. Of course Don Rodrigo didn't want her out there, in the midst of people over whom he had no control. 'Where were you accepted?' he asked.

'Oxford and the Sorbonne.'

He looked at her, brows raised. 'That's pretty good.'

'You seem surprised,' she countered, challenging him. 'I suppose it's because I'm a woman?'

'Guilty,' he said, a new and delicious twinkle brightening his eyes. 'I'm afraid I'm not used to coming across women who are as lovely as you and yet who are obviously also highly gifted and intelligent.'

Nena's cheeks flushed and she looked quickly away. 'Oh, I'm not really that bright. I just like studying, that's all. There's the wood,' she mumbled hastily.

'What about your boyfriend?' he probed. 'Does he want you to go to university?'

'Boyfriend?' Nena frowned again, then laughed, a natural spontaneous gurgle that left Ramon swallowing. 'Oh, I see. No, I don't have a boyfriend. Well, I have friends, of course, like Jimmy Chandler and David Onslow at the tennis club, but that's different.'

'And have none of them ever tried to kiss you?' he asked in an amused, bantering tone, unable to resist the temptation of finding out more about this alluring creature to whom he was becoming increasingly drawn, despite the strange situation they were in.

'Oh, Lord, no—they're just pals.' Nena gave an embarrassed shrug and their eyes met as they reached the edge of the wood. 'This is the wood. Do you want to see it?'

'Honestly?' His eyes flashed wickedly.

'Honestly,' she responded, lips twitching.

'Honestly, I have no interest whatsoever in seeing your wood—though if it is half as charming as its owner I suppose I should.'

'Oh, shut up.' She giggled, feeling now as though she'd known him a while. 'That's totally silly.'

'Why don't we sit over there by the lake for a few minutes and relax?'

'All right.'

They walked back across the bridge and down to the water's edge. 'Here, let me lay this on the grass; it may be damp,' he said, spreading out his jacket for her, trying to sort out the conflict raging in his mind.

'Thanks.' She sat on part of the jacket, leaving room for him, and he lowered himself next to her.

'Tell me, what's it like living with your grandfather?' he asked suddenly, throwing a pebble spinning into the still waters of the lake.

'I love him dearly. I mean, of course at times it's a bit restrictive, but I need to look after him. That's why I didn't tell him I'd been accepted at Oxford, or he might have changed his mind and felt obliged to let me go. Then there would have been no one to look after him.'

'But surely the staff would take care of him?'

'Yes, but that's not the same at all,' she dismissed, raising her lovely determined chin. 'Lately he seems to be so frail. I can't quite explain it, but...' She hesitated and pressed her fingers together, a sudden frown creasing her brow. 'I'm just being silly, I suppose, but it worries me.' She looked up and their eyes met. 'Your parents seem so nice,' she said, changing the subject. 'Do you live with them or on your own?'

'Oh, on my own. I have several houses—my *hacienda,* a loft in Puert Madero in Buenos Aires. In London I stay at my parents' place in Eaton Square, though. Quite a change,' he added, aware that he could hardly tell her that he shared his life with Luisa, his official mistress, and on occasion a smattering of models, who drifted in and out. Luisa was not officially in-house, of course, but it was an ongoing relationship. And although she knew he had no intention of marrying her—she was twice divorced—they had a very pleasant time together.

Which brought him back to the matter at hand. What would happen to Luisa if, by some twist of fate, he decided to accept Don Rodrigo's proposition?

Ramon glanced down at Nena once more. She was lovely, and unaware of it. Just as she was unaware of what awaited her just around the corner. Her grandfather's death would shake her for ever from the safe cocoon she'd lived in all her life. It would be harsh and painful, he realised sadly. For as an only grandchild she was probably even more protected from the world than if her parents had been alive. Also she'd have no one—except some friends and her financial advisors—to turn to. Perhaps, he reflected sombrely, Don Rodrigo was not so wrong to want to protect her from all that might be waiting for her out there. All at once Ramon shared the old man's fears for her.

'Maybe we should be getting back,' he said abruptly, glancing at the thin gold watch on his tanned wrist. 'My parents will be wanting to leave soon.'

'All right.' She jumped up and he picked up the jacket, throwing it over his shoulder again as they made their way back to the group on the lawn.

It was odd, he reflected, that a plan which only an hour ago had struck him as absolutely preposterous now seemed considerably less so. Plus, as both Don Rodrigo and his father had pointed out, it was a marriage, not an affair. He was thirty-two, and would have to think of marriage and a family shortly anyway. Wouldn't it be infinitely preferable to be married to a lovely creature like Nena, whom he could mould to his liking, teach the art of love, yet continue enjoying the Luisas of this world on the side? he reflected somewhat ruthlessly. All in all, having a beautiful, well-mannered society wife, whom he could take pleasure with in bed from time to time without changing his routine, might not be such a bad thing after all.

'My love, I have something I need to speak to you about,' Don Rodrigo said to his granddaughter the next evening over dinner.

'Yes, Grandfather?' Nena looked at him closely. He seemed very tired. In the past few days he had barely left his room, except to sit on the lawn yesterday afternoon with the Villalbas. 'Is something wrong?' she enquired anxiously.

'After dinner we shall retire to the study and have a chat,' he said, knowing the moment had finally arrived when he must tell her the truth.

Since the acceptance that morning of the proposition of marriage by Ramon Villalba he had known it was essential she learn about his illness and what the future held, however painful.

Don Rodrigo sampled a tiny spoonful of chocolate mousse. It turned bitter on his tongue. He had faced many hard moments in his life, but telling this child whom he loved so dearly that the end was near would rank among the cruellest blows life had dealt him. His only solace was that Ramon Villalba had, for whatever reason, accepted his proposition.

Half an hour later, seated as always on the tapestried footstool at his feet, Nena listened in anguished horror to her grandfather's words.

'But that's impossible,' she cried, grabbing his hands and squeezing them tight. 'It can't be true, Grandfather, there must be a mistake. You must have other tests—other opinions. It simply can't be right,' she ended, sobbing.

'I'm afraid I've already done all that,' he responded sadly, stroking the mane of tawny hair fanned out on his lap and soothing her tears. 'That is why I have had to make provision for you.'

'Pro-provision?' she gulped, raising her head, still trying to absorb the horrible news he'd imparted.

'Yes, my love. You must be taken care of, provided for.'

'Please, Grandfather, don't talk about it,' she sobbed.

'I'm afraid I must. Time is short and measures must be taken.'

'Wh-what measures?' she gulped sadly, trying to regain some control as the truth sank in.

Don Rodrigo hesitated, then, with a sigh, forged ahead. 'Yesterday you met Ramon Villalba.'

'Yes,' she whispered, taking his handkerchief and blowing her nose hard.

'And you found him—pleasant?'

'Yes, I suppose so. He was polite. Look, Grandfather, what has that got to do with you being ill?' she burst out, leaning back on her heels, eyes pleading.

'Ramon Villalba has proposed marriage.'

'Marriage?' Nena let out a horrified gasp and stood up, clutching the damp handkerchief between her nervous fingers. 'But that is absurd, Grandfather. How

can I get married to a man I don't know, whom I
don't love? I don't want to get married. I—'

'Shush, child, do not get so agitated. Come here.'
He held out his hand and she sank once more to the
footstool. 'I have talked to the Villalbas. We all agree
that this marriage is a good thing.'

'How—how can you say that, Grandfather? It's archaic. Nobody is forced to marry any longer; it's un-
heard of. Oh, please, Grandfather, this can't be real.
There must be a mistake. I'm sure if you went to
another doctor—'

'Now, now. I want you to listen, Nena. Carefully.
I am absolutely decided on this marriage. And I want
the wedding to take place as soon as possible.'

'You mean he came here to inspect me, as he might
a horse or a piece of cattle?' she cried. 'Why would
he propose an arrangement like this?'

'I can think of several reasons—all of them perfectly valid,' Don Rodrigo answered firmly. 'He
needs a wife from a good family and of excellent
upbringing who is unsoiled. Also he is adequately
prepared to take care of our business ventures.'

'So that's it,' she whispered bitterly. 'A business
arrangement. Oh, Grandfather, how can you auction
me off like this? It's all too horrible.' She turned, and
her shoulders shook as she sobbed. Her pain at learn-
ing of her grandfather's terminal illness was somehow
increased by the knowledge that a man whom she'd
ended the afternoon finding most agreeable was in
fact nothing but a dirtbag. 'You talked with him without knowing if I wanted this?' she whispered at last,
turning back to him, her eyes glistening with tears.

'Yes, Nena, I did. Villalba is a practical man. I
have informed myself, followed his career over a pe-

riod of several years. He will take care of you, look out for you and the fortune you are going to inherit.'

'I don't care about any of that!' she exclaimed.

'Maybe not, but I do. Please do this for me,' he added, a softer, pleading note entering his voice. 'I can die in peace knowing that you are in his hands.'

'Oh, please don't talk like that,' she begged once more, kneeling next to him.

'Then agree to my request,' Don Rodrigo said, exercising a considerable amount of emotional pressure. He sighed inwardly. It was the only way to bring the matter to a fast and satisfactory conclusion. 'Answer me, Nena. Tell me you'll do as I ask.'

Nena stared through her tears at the carpet, her emotions in turmoil. The last thing she wanted was to be married to a man she barely knew. A wave of frustration overtook her. This was, after all, the most important step in her life—yet she had no control over it. Despite her feelings, she already knew what the answer must be.

'I'll do it, Grandfather,' she whispered.

At that moment she hated Ramon Villalba.

CHAPTER TWO

THE wedding—a small, intimate affair, with only the two families present—took place at the fashionable church of St James, Spanish Place, in London, two weeks later. Afterwards they returned to Don Rodrigo's house in Chester Square to quietly celebrate the nuptials.

Nena wafted through the ceremony in a daze, her emotions blunted, the pain of seeing her grandfather withering daily barely allowing her to think clearly about what the future next to a man she despised would hold.

'Are you okay?' Ramon asked quietly, touching her arm as they moved into the hall. She deposited the bouquet of flowers on the hall table and allowed the butler to take her wrap.

'I'm perfectly all right,' she answered coldly.

'Are you sure?' He looked down at her, noting the dark rings around her beautiful green eyes and the sadness they held. 'A bride should be happy on her wedding day.'

'Happy?' she jeered, sending him a glare. 'How could any bride be happy, married in these circumstances?'

'I know these are not the happiest of times,' he agreed levelly, glancing at Don Rodrigo, mounting the stairs with extreme difficulty. 'Still, I want you to know, Nena, that as your husband I shall do my best to make you happy.'

'How very gracious of you,' she responded bitterly, barely attempting to conceal the anger in her voice. How dared he pretend he cared? Wasn't it bad enough that she was losing her grandfather, whom she adored, without having Ramon's odious presence thrust upon her?

She sent him an angry look, then spun on the heel of her designer shoe and marched towards the stairs.

Ramon followed her at a distance. To his consternation Nena had not unbent, as he'd hoped she would. She had refused to receive him again before the wedding and had barely addressed a word to him since leaving the church. He sighed. This did not bode well for the future. But it was done now. The knot had been tied and the vows exchanged. All that remained was for them both to make the best of it.

'I thought you would prefer to come here to the island rather than be with a crowd,' Ramon said above the purr of the engine as the helicopter hovered over the Aegean.

Nena could distinguish an island below, and a small port, with a yacht and a number of colourful fishing boats bobbing in the harbour. Then she saw a rambling white villa, surrounded by smaller dwellings with little blue shutters and, in the distance, a windmill. At any other time she would have been enchanted. But right now being in Greece on her bridegroom's private island or being in Battersea would have meant about the same to her. All she wanted was to be alone, to think, to assimilate the shock that having her world tipped topsy-turvy from one moment to the other had left her in.

As they alighted Ramon took her hand firmly, and they walked up a small winding path from the beach where the chopper had landed. A soft evening breeze blew in from the sea, gulls twirled overhead, and villagers sat on the wall waving at them with bright smiles. As they approached the villa a little girl ran forward and, curtseying, handed her a bouquet of wild flowers. Despite her numb state and her sadness, Nena smiled down at the child and thanked her.

She gazed at the flowers, reminded that this was her wedding day.

The saddest day of her life.

For a moment tears welled, but she suppressed them as fast as they came. She had no right to be unhappy. At least her grandfather would have a happy end to his life. And that mattered more than anything.

Then all at once she became deeply conscious of Ramon standing next to her, his powerful body so close he almost touched her. And she shivered. What came next in this awful sequence of events? she wondered as slowly they moved on up towards the steps of the house. What would he expect from her as his wife?

For the first time, as they entered the huge hall, then stepped into the tiled drawing room and out onto the low-walled terrace overlooking the cerulean sea beyond, Nena faced her dilemma. Suddenly she glanced at Ramon, who was speaking to one of the servants. He looked like a man not used to being thwarted. Everyone jumped at his quiet, polite commands. What, she wondered, would he want from her?

'I've ordered some champagne,' he said, looking

down at her. 'Afterwards you might like to tour the first of your new homes,' he added, with that same touch of sardonic humour she'd observed the first day by the lake. *Remember,* she told herself, *he doesn't care about you. You're nothing more than a lucrative asset.*

'I feel rather tired,' she said, seating herself on the colourful woven cushions that were spread over the white-washed stone sofa surrounding the wall that formed a cozy niche. 'I think I'll go and rest in a minute, if you don't mind. Perhaps one of the maids could show me to my room.'

'To *our* room, you mean,' he returned firmly.

Her eyes flew up to meet his and she shivered. 'I—I think we need to talk about that.' She clasped her hands together and felt her cheeks go bright pink.

'What is there to talk about?' Ramon asked, leaning lazily back against the wall in his immaculate grey suit. He managed to look at ease in it, despite being on a relaxed Greek island.

'A lot, I think.'

'Oh?' He raised an enquiring brow.

'Yes. We—this is a marriage of convenience. You, for whatever reason, decided that it suited you to propose,' she replied hotly, sending him an angry glare. 'I accepted because I love my grandfather and don't want him to end his days worrying and miserable. I don't think that either of those reasons constitutes grounds for—for intimacy.' She ended hurriedly, wishing this conversation wasn't taking place.

'I see.' Ramon gazed at her speculatively. He hadn't reckoned with this—had thought that once he had her to himself things would somehow smooth themselves out. Perhaps, he reflected reluctantly, he would have to give her some time to get used to the idea that she was his.

The thought sent a slash of heat racing through his body and he stood straighter. 'We'll talk about this later on,' he said, seeing a servant appear with the champagne. 'For now, let's relax and have a drink.'

Seconds later he was handing her a glass filled with sparkling champagne. 'Welcome to Agapos,' he said, raising his glass. 'May you be happy and contented here, *señora mia.*'

Nena made a minute gesture of acknowledgement with her glass, and instead of the sip she'd intended took a large, long gulp. She certainly needed something to get her through the next few hours…days— nights.

Ramon watched her. He would have to restrain the desire that had been consuming him for the past two weeks and control the powerful urge he had to take her to his bed. There was time for that, he told himself. No need to rush things. He was willing to pander to her present needs—for a while. Still, there was a limit to his patience.

But she was experiencing a period of deep trauma, caused by her grandfather's illness, and their marriage must have come as something of a surprise, he realised soberly. Then there was the fact that she was very young, and apparently had very little or no sexual experience. She was perhaps afraid. It would be up to him to make sure that it all happened smoothly, that her initiation to the bedroom and its pleasures was an enjoyable experience. He took a deep breath and forced his mind onto something else before his body betrayed him.

*   *   *

Three nights later Ramon was feeling considerably less amenable. Nena had barely spoken to him, and when she did she was grudgingly polite. They'd spent several stonily silent hours on the beach, on the yacht, driving around the island. If he proposed a plan she agreed neither happily nor unhappily.

Indifferent.

That was what she was. And it was driving him crazy. He could have handled raw anger, tears, a show of passion. But this blatant unresponsiveness and determination to remain as distant from him as possible was intolerable.

He sent her a scorching glance across the table which had been tastefully laid on the terrace. The moon was rising and the night was dotted with stars. The perfect night to be with a woman, he thought. They could have spent wonderful hours together, yet she refused to budge from this tenacious position she'd assumed. What was going on inside that lovely head? he wondered. What thoughts rankled? What was it that was eating her?

'Nena, I think that if there is something disturbing you, you should tell me about it. I've tried to be as accommodating as possible,' he added, thinking of the separate bedrooms he'd instructed the staff to arrange, 'but I think you owe me an explanation.'

'An explanation?' She lowered her fork to her plate and sent an icy stare across the crisp white cloth. 'I don't think I owe you anything, Ramon. Neither of us owes the other. We cut a deal. We each, apparently—though I don't quite see it that way—are supposed to benefit from this arrangement. I can see the advantages for you. I have yet to find out what mine are.'

'Is that how you see this? Purely as a business arrangement?' he said, shocked that someone so young could be so level-headed, so...

'That's exactly how I think of it. And the sooner you do so as well, the better it will be for both of us. Why don't we end this farce of a honeymoon at once and get back home?'

'We are home,' he replied coldly. 'Home, from now on, is where I reside. My homes have now become your homes.'

'I have to go back to my grandfather,' she said doggedly staring at her plate.

'I have no objection to remaining in England for the present. But in our home.'

'But—'

'There are no buts,' he returned autocratically. 'We shall stay with my parents. I have instructed my estate agents to look for a place for us.'

'I don't want to go to Eaton Square,' Nena muttered through gritted teeth, her fingers clenched as she tried not to cry. 'I want to go home—to Thurston. Why don't you just go back to Buenos Aires and—?'

She stopped herself in time from saying *back to your mistress*. He had no idea that she'd seen the pictures of him and Luisa Somebody-or-other in *Hola!* magazine. The pictures had been taken in Gstaad, where they'd been winter sporting. In fact Ramon had no notion that she knew about his lifestyle. She had found out quite by chance about the woman in his life, as she'd flipped through an old copy of the magazine that Doña Augusta had brought for her grandfather.

And, surprisingly, it had hurt.

It didn't matter that she despised the man for agreeing to marry her, despised his motives and everything he stood for. The sight of him—arm possessively around the shoulders of a lush, luscious, stunning brunette, obviously a highly worldly and sophisticated woman, near to his own age—had left her inordinately troubled. Not that it was anything to do with her, she'd reasoned then as she did now. What did she care how many women he slept with? She had no intention of being one of them, did she?

Ramon leaned forward and touched her hand. 'Nena, I have no objection to your visiting your grandfather, spending time with him, and of course there will come a time—' He cut off, unwilling to say the words he knew would hurt her so much, while deeply aware that it was his duty to prepare her for what he suspected would take place in a very short time. 'But I do require that your official and permanent residence be under my roof,' he finished firmly as she drew her trembling fingers from his grasp. 'I will not allow my wife to live anywhere but with me.'

He'd never thought he would feel so strongly possessive the day he married. Had never thought about it much at all. But now that it had happened he felt a need to control, to be in the driving seat. He had never bothered being jealous in the past. If a woman lost interest—why, he usually had long before, and was sticking around out of courtesy.

But Nena was different. He sensed it deep down in a part of himself he hadn't known existed, some deep, primeval instinct that he'd tapped into on his wedding day and wouldn't leave him be; the same instinct that was leaving him ever more antsy as he passed her closed door each night on his way to bed.

Patience, he repeated to himself once again. She's young. Give her time. But it was becoming increasingly difficult.

That night Nena was unable to sleep. She had slipped on one of the beautiful, flimsy, spaghetti-strapped lawn nightdresses that were part of her hastily put together trousseau, chosen by her personal shopper. She looked down at it and sighed. She'd taken no interest in her trousseau, had merely agreed with anything Maureen had shown her. Now, half-afraid, she looked at herself in the mirror. She could see the shadow of her body peeping through the thin fabric and closed her eyes. How hard it was to admit to herself that despite her wish to alienate him, she was constantly thinking of her husband, that when he came close to her every nerve vibrated, that a new, torrid heat she'd never known charged through her being with an alien vibrance that left her damp in places she was embarrassed to think of. Desperately she searched for answers, unable to pinpoint this new, unquenchable thirst that had invaded her being and couldn't be satiated.

Angry with herself, and desperate to be in the open, she moved out onto the vast balcony that contoured the upper story of the villa. Leaning her hands on the balustrade, her long hair flowing about her shoulders, Nena gazed out over the Aegean at the starlit night and listened to the sea softly lapping the shore. This was her honeymoon, and should have been the most wonderful moment of her life, yet here she was, miserable in more ways than one. She let out a long sigh.

'Aren't you sleepy?' The deep husky voice just behind her made her spin round and gasp, another thrust of emotion rushing through her.

Ramon stood before her, more handsome than ever in silk pyjama pants, the top open revealing an expanse of bronzed chest. In the pool of lantern light she could see a gleam flashing in his golden-flecked chestnut eyes as they flicked over her, taking in each detail of her body in a cool, possessive manner, as an owner might look over a thoroughbred. The thin nightdress, she knew, left little to the imagination.

Ashamed, Nena moved her hands behind her against the balustrade, unaware that by doing so her small, delicious breasts were thrust towards him invitingly as her hair fell back from her shoulders and her perfect throat glistened in the moonlight.

God, she was lovely, Ramon acknowledged, a shaft of untamed desire taking hold once more as he moved towards her, unable to resist. And she was his wife. He had every right to possess her.

'Nena,' he whispered, his voice low and sultry, 'let me love you. Let me be your husband.'

'I—I can't—' she responded hoarsely, only too conscious of his scent, of the maleness of him, of everything about him that drew her even while she tried desperately to remind herself of all the reasons why she couldn't let it happen.

'I promise not to hurt you,' he said reasonably, leaning his hands on each side of the balustrade, his tanned face and sensual lips only inches from hers.

It was then Nena realised, with a tingling shudder that left her weak, that he was about to kiss her.

And she could do nothing to stop him. Knew that however much she tried to justify it to herself she wouldn't stop him. She must resist, must not show

him that she cared, that in spite of the fact that she
despised him she also longed for his touch, to discover
in his arms what it would be like to become a woman.

Then, before she could think further, his lips came
down on hers, and Nena gave way to her first real
kiss. She felt his lips prying hers open. For a moment
she tried to draw back and protest, but the firm yet
gentle insistence of his tongue working its way cun-
ningly into her mouth, left her clutching his hard
shoulders instead, trying to hold on to something as
the earth swayed beneath her feet.

Ramon drew her into his arms, and, pressing his hand
into the small of her back, felt the delicious curve of
her bottom, her small taut breasts pressed against his
chest. What would she do when she felt his hardness
against her? he wondered. He was careful not to rush
her as his tongue probed further, thrusting carefully,
leading her gently to a response, containing his rampant
desire to possess her until she was ready for more,
aware that this was her first everything.

So he took it slowly, sensing her waning resistance,
the fight between her brain and her body, her instinct
and her soul. Then, just as smoothly and firmly, he
drew her closer—until she could feel the length of
him, until her tongue began tentatively seeking his,
guiding her all the way, hands caressing her back, the
soft curve of her perfect thighs.

Then all at once he felt her arms tighten about him,
heard her tiny gasp as he left her mouth and began
kissing her throat, and knew he was well on his way.

Nena threw her head back and moaned, giving herself up to his caresses. She let out another tiny gasp
of delight and surprise when his lips reached her
breast, encircling her taut nipple, taunting it through

the soft texture of her nightdress, making her want to scream with joy and pain, to reach for more, to feel free of the fabric that stood between them. But still Ramon lingered.

Slipping a hand from behind her, he gently fondled her other breast until Nena thought she couldn't bear the searing rush of heat that stabbed her somewhere down in a place she'd never been entirely conscious of until this moment, but that now begged for some new kind of fulfilment and release.

Then a primal, tight, knotted spiral that she'd never before experienced rose within her, mounting until she thought she'd scream. And just as she could bear it no longer, as her fingers raked his thick black hair and she wanted to beg for mercy, for him to stop, a miracle happened and the hot, intense, coiled build-up crashed, simply let loose, wafted into an ecstatic joyride that lingered on and on for several seconds, leaving her limp and weak, her knees giving way beneath her as Ramon held her up and she fell extenuated against him.

'Mi linda,' he whispered, lifting her in his arms then carrying her through the French windows into his bedroom with the male satisfaction and pride of knowing he'd just introduced her to her first sexual experience.

'What happened?' she whispered as he laid her down in the middle of the huge bamboo four-poster bed, with its voile curtains and soft, cool linen sheets.

'You just experienced your first orgasm,' he said, slipping next to her onto the bed, his smile as arrogant as it was possessive.

'Oh.' Slowly Nena recouped her breath. Then suddenly she became aware that Ramon was about to remove his pyjama pants. Exercising every ounce of will-power, she sat up and brushed her hair aside, little aware of how tantalising she looked in the glow of the soft bedside lamps.

'Ramon, what are you doing?'

'Nena, you may be young and a virgin,' he said with a touch of humour in his flashing brown eyes, 'but I think you know very well what I'm doing. It's time I made you truly my wife.'

'No. I don't want to.' She moved back against the pillows and drew her legs up under her nightdress.

'Nena, after what just happened out there that is a ridiculous statement,' he said with a low, husky laugh that left her once again prey to the rush of heat that had assailed her previously. 'You want me just as much as I want you,' he said softly, trailing his long dark fingers from her throat to her breast, where he stopped just above her nipple and looked deep into her eyes. 'Tell me you don't want me to start all over again,' he said with quiet, yet arrogant assurance, 'and I'll leave you alone.'

Nena tried to think straight, to resist the tantalising caress that was fuzzing her brain. 'I don't—I can't—'

'Yes, you can, *mi linda,* of course you can. Remember, I'm your husband. You can do anything with me, Nena, anything at all. I'll show you, take you places you've never dreamed of.'

Her better judgement now fading into complete oblivion, Nena let her head sink back against the pillow with a long sigh.

'No,' Ramon said in an authoritative tone, 'don't run away from me. I want you here with me. I want you to know who is loving you and when. Nena, take off your nightgown.'

Again she tried to shy away. 'No. Please, Ramon, I—'

'Nena, might I remind you that a few days ago you vowed to obey me? I would hate to see you not keep your word.' His eyes pinned her now, allowing no room for flight. 'I am your husband, the man who has the right to see you, to possess you.'

It was a command, she realised, wishing she had the will-power to refuse him. Part of her hated him for what he was doing; the other submitted with intense female surrender. After all, he was right. The vow to obey had been part of their marriage ceremony; she had pronounced the words. But she hadn't thought of their meaning. Now, seeing him rise and stand over her next to the bed, his face unsmiling as his gaze held hers, she knew that the words were for real.

Slowly, very slowly, Nena slipped to the edge of the bed.

'Stand up,' he ordered softly.

Nena did as he bade her—standing, cheeks flushed, clenching her hands, as gently but firmly he pulled up the nightdress and slipped it over her head, leaving her before him with nothing but the long strands of her silky tawny mane for protection.

Then Ramon took a step back and feasted his eyes on her. 'You're beautiful—lovely,' he whispered hoarsely, letting his fingers trail over her, past her breast on down to her belly.

Despite her embarrassment Nena experienced another mind-wrenching tingle rush through her when his fingers reached further. All at once she realised she felt damp and hot, filled with a desire so great she could barely control the moan that escaped her when his fingers fondled her soft mound of golden curls, then slipped between her legs, probing further as he drew her close with his other arm.

And all at once she wanted to experience his skin on hers, to know what he felt like, and it was she who began tugging at the tie of his pyjamas.

'Not so fast, *cariña,*' he murmured, close to her ear. 'There's time for that.'

'No,' she muttered, gasping as he touched a place deep inside her, provoking thrusts of pain and joy, leaving her increasingly ragged and wanting. 'You saw me. Now I want to see you.'

Ramon let out a low, satisfied laugh. 'Very well, my darling.' With that he continued caressing her with one hand while with the other he helped her remove the offending garments.

Soon they were standing naked, facing one another. Then Ramon gently removed his fingers and looked into her eyes. 'I am your husband, Nena, don't be ashamed.'

And the amazing thing, Nena realised, baffled, was that she wasn't. In fact she felt a strange new power take hold as he looked at her, and—tentatively at first—she allowed herself to look at his body, feast on his strong, bronzed and muscled limbs, his broad yet lean torso, then on down.

Firmly Ramon slipped his hand over hers and drew it towards him. 'I want you to feel me as I've felt you,' he said, drawing her back into his arms and gently placing her hand upon him, strangely enchanted to know that this was the first time she'd been with a man, that he was the first to teach her. Another

sudden rush of possessiveness and then something far
stronger hit him with utter surprise: for all at once he
hoped he would be the last.

It was a strange, overwhelming feeling that left him
more emotionally touched than he could have believed possible. Now, as his arms slipped around her
once more and he drew her back onto the bed, he
tried to reason with himself, keep up the control. But
he couldn't—could think only of reaching further,
knowing her thoroughly, and he kissed her, not
gently, as before, but with a new, surging passion that
eradicated all trace of hesitation. The latter was replaced by a passionate, gnawing hunger that he'd
rarely known but that needed to be assuaged.

Nena held her breath and let her feelings take over,
her heart beating so loudly she was sure he would
hear it, delighting in the hard wall of muscled male
body cleaving against her. And something more,
something much more troubling yet stirring, a primal
need, grew inside her that she knew she had to pursue,
as Ramon began a thorough and delicious investigation of her body, starting with feathery kisses at her
throat that descended, further and further, taunting her
aching swollen nipples, then moved on down until he
reached her core.

Nena let out a gasp as his tongue flicked over the
little nub of sensitive flesh she'd been unaware existed until this very moment. Seconds later she was
moaning, writhing, unable to restrain the need to rake
her fingers through his hair.

'Ramon!' she cried, and shattered again into a myriad of indescribable sensations, only to end up curled
in his arms as he whispered sweet nothings in her ear

and soothed her gently as every pulse in her body beat wildly.

And there was more to come.

Just as Nena was beginning to steady herself Ramon slipped his fingers between her thighs once more and probed, slowly, feeling the soft liquid honey, making sure she was ready for what was to happen next.

'Nena, *mi amor,*' he whispered huskily. 'I'm going to make you mine, all mine.' His almost imperceptible Spanish lilt thickened with passion as firmly he slid on top of her and parted her thighs.

Nena felt her body tense.

'Don't be afraid, *querida.* I'll do my best not to hurt you.'

'I—I've never—'

'I know, *corazon,* just leave it to me.' He dropped a long kiss on her mouth and at the same time eased himself gently into her.

Nena experienced a moment's shock as she felt him reach within her, just a little at first, as though letting her get used to the novelty. Then all at once he penetrated further. Nena gave a gasp of pain when he thrust deep, and dug her nails into his shoulders.

'It's all right, *mi amor,*' he murmured softly, his kisses almost reverent in their gentleness, his eyes dark and bright and filled with a gleam she didn't recognise. And the pain was quickly replaced by another of those lingering, rising coils of desire. At each new thrust Nena felt herself arching involuntarily towards him, her hips moving in a new and wonderful cadence. Then all became hazy, fuzzy, as she felt him join her, knew that he was somehow experiencing the same incredible sensation she was. And together they

soared, swept away on a powerful, forceful wave of
passion so strong that when it came to their climax
they cried together, then fell exhausted onto the rumpled sheets, too spent to do more than listen to the
beat of each other's hearts.

CHAPTER THREE

'DON RAMON?'

After several knocks Ramon awoke and realised that Juanito, his manservant, who'd accompanied he and Nena on the honeymoon, was outside the door, urgently calling his name.

Rising quickly from the rumpled bed, Ramon pulled on his discarded pyjama pants and dragged his fingers through his hair. He glanced down at Nena, still fast asleep, curled up like a kitten under the sheet, her hair fanned over the pillow, and smiled before he turned and went to the door. Opening it carefully, so as not to wake her, he slipped into the corridor.

'What is it, Juanito?' he asked, smothering a yawn. *'Que pasa?'*

'It is Don Rodrigo, *señor. Doña* Augusta called to advise you that he has taken a turn for the worse. She and Don Pedro feel you should return to London immediately.'

'My God.' Ramon was fully awake now, his mind working nineteen to the dozen. He glanced at the door. How would she react? he wondered, heart sinking, knowing he would have to go back into the room, wake Nena from her slumber and tell her the devastating news.

'*Muy bien,*' he said with a firm nod. 'See that the chopper is here within the hour, and tell the pilot to have the plane ready for take-off. We should be at Athens International Airport shortly.'

With that he turned on his heel and faced the daunting task of telling the woman to whom he had made love last night, for the first time, that the honeymoon he'd begun to have such hopes for was about to end. He entered, watched her, still curled up on the bed, then moved towards it. He sat down on the edge, next to her, face softening as his fingers gently smoothed the amazing mane of hair that was neither dark nor light, but a unique shade, highlighted with a myriad of golden streaks.

Bracing himself, he dropped a light kiss on her eyelids, then her mouth.

'Nena,' he whispered, gently shaking her shoulder, 'You must wake up, *cariña.*'

Slowly, very slowly, Nena emerged from a delicious dream. At first she kept her eyes closed, still basking in the aftermath of a wonderful night's sleep. Then all at once she stretched, became conscious of her body, of a slight pain when she moved, and little by little she recalled and pieced together the events of the night before.

Opening her eyes with a start, she looked up into Ramon's face.

'Good morning, *señora mia,*' he said softly. 'How did you sleep?' There was a gleam in his eyes as he spoke, and Nena felt her cheeks warm as in a sudden instant the lovemaking of the previous evening flashed before her.

'Fi-fine,' she muttered, looking away as Ramon leaned down and slipped an arm under her, drawing her close.

'Don't be embarrassed by what occurred between us, *mi linda,*' he said cajolingly, 'it is how it should be.'

He did not add that he'd been struck by the intensity of feeling that had hit him when at last he'd penetrated her fully and made her his. He had never experienced anything quite so powerful. And there had been women in his life, many women—younger ones, older ones—all of them exciting experiences who had taught him to perfect the art of lovemaking, of becoming a skilled and thoughtful lover as well as satisfying his own needs. But never before had he experienced such sheer, unadulterated passion as he had with his virgin wife.

But now was not the moment to be thinking of those things, he reminded himself, regretting that he couldn't prolong the aftermath and start all over again. Duty, after all, came first.

Pulling her gently to a sitting position, careful to help her wrap the sheet decorously about her, he placed his hands on her shoulders. 'Nena, I'm afraid I have some bad news.'

'Oh? What is it?' She frowned, fully awake now, her eyes wide with sudden fear.

'I'm afraid it's your grandfather. He's taken a turn for the worse.'

'Oh, no!' She pulled back from him and gazed up in horror. 'I must go at once,' she whispered, suddenly aware that here she was, making love with this man who'd been thrust upon her and whom she'd allowed to take possession of her body, when her grandfather was lying ill and probably needing her. 'I must leave!' she cried, struggling to get up.

Ramon rose quickly, leaving her room to move. 'I have arranged for the chopper to be here shortly.'

'Thank you,' she replied stiffly, rising, the sheet wrapped around her like a toga. 'I shall be ready.'

'Right, then we'll leave as soon as it lands.'

'We?'

'Of course,' he responded haughtily.

'But I can go alone,' Nena said, suddenly anguished at the thought of having him along, wanting to be by herself, to try and forget the shame she was experiencing.

How could she have allowed last night to happen? How could she have forgotten her grandfather and let herself be sucked into Ramon's bed and—? Oh! It was all too awful, and too frustrating. This man, after all, wanted nothing from her but to own her—make her part of his already vast array of possessions. And now he'd branded her, asserted his ownership, and he probably imagined he could take her whenever he wanted, use her to satisfy his needs, like the rest of his belongings.

Gathering together some last shreds of dignity, Nena nodded curtly, head high, and moved towards the huge marble bathroom she perceived through the half-open door. But even the hot jet of water blasting her from the shower didn't erase the tormented and uneasy feelings of guilt and shame that assailed her.

Ramon sighed as she closed the door behind her.

He could read her like a book—the doubts, the anger, the shock, the self-recrimination written in her eyes— and wished only that there was time to help assuage some of the inevitable emotions she was experiencing. But he shrugged and made his way to the other bathroom of the suite. Priorities came first. He must get her back to Don Rodrigo as soon as possible.

And he hoped desperately that it wouldn't be too late.

Nena barely spoke a word during the flight back to London. When they arrived at Heathrow customs officers came quickly on board and formalities were rapidly dealt with. Then they climbed into Ramon's Bentley, waiting on the tarmac to pick them up, and roared off immediately towards Windsor.

Several calls on Ramon's mobile phone had kept them abreast of Don Rodrigo's progress, which was not good. He would very probably be moved to hospital if he didn't improve by the afternoon.

Nena sat in the corner of the leather seat, as far from Ramon as possible, and clasped her hands in her lap, hating herself. How would she ever forgive herself for not being here when her grandfather had most needed her? She should never have consented to the wretched honeymoon in the first place—should have been more attentive to all the arrangements. In fact she simply should have refused. They could easily have stayed somewhere nearby. There had been no need to go all the way to Greece.

Over and over she chastised herself, so that by the time they arrived at Thurston Manor she was jumping out of the car before the chauffeur could so much as open the door.

As Ramon alighted he watched her burst into the house and run up the stairs towards her grandfather's apartments, heedless of the nurse and Doña Augusta standing in the corridor.

It was only when she finally reached the door of his room that she slowed down, took a deep breath, straightened her hair, then opened it quietly and tip-toed in, so as not to disturb the patient.

The room was dark, the curtains closed to keep out the glaring sunlight. Don Rodrigo lay very still in the middle of the large oak bed. He seemed so much smaller, frailer than when she had last seen him. And as she approached the bed Nena stifled a sob before slipping soundlessly into the chair next to it. Gently she laid her hand on his wax-like one, lying motion-less on the coverlet.

'I'm here, Grandfather,' she whispered softly, a sob catching in her throat. 'Please forgive me for having been away when you needed me.'

'Nena?' Slowly the old eyes opened and his head moved stiffly on the pillow. 'Ah, my child, you are here.' He closed them again and squeezed her hand weakly. 'So silly of me to get worse just at the mo-ment,' he added in a faint voice.

'Oh, Grandfather, I'm sure that now you'll get bet-ter!' Nena exclaimed, passing her hand over his brow, determined that somehow she would make him re-cover, despite the doctor's dire prognosis.

Don Rodrigo managed a dim smile. 'Ah, my Nena.

You were always such a sweet, determined little thing,' he whispered.

Just then the door opened, and she looked up to see Doña Augusta and Ramon enter, followed by the middle-aged uniformed nurse.

'I'm afraid he mustn't get too tired,' the nurse said gently, coming forward with a tray. 'If you would excuse us, Mrs Villalba? I need to give Don Rodrigo his medication.'

Nena experienced a jolt at being called Mrs Villalba. Since their marriage they'd been on the island, and the servants had addressed her as Doña Nena or Kiria Nena, in Greek. It was similar to the way she'd been addressed during her many stays in Argentina. Now the truth of her situation and all its implications sank in as never before.

'Very well,' she said, rising and dropping a kiss on her grandfather's withered brow. 'I'll be back later, darling,' she whispered.

He nodded faintly, but she could see that already he looked paler, that even the few minutes spent with her had exhausted him.

Biting her lip, she turned without so much as a glance at her husband and left the room.

Doña Augusta took her arm. 'I'm so sorry, Nena,' she said, slipping her hand over the young girl's, pained to see her suffering so intensely. 'Now, come downstairs and have a cup of tea or a drink. You need it. Your grandfather is getting the best possible care.'

Nena merely nodded. Her mind was full of so many troubled thoughts that she could barely concentrate on what her mother-in-law was saying. Once they were in the drawing room she remained vaguely aware of Ramon, standing near the fireplace, his mouth set in a hard line and a frown creasing his thick dark brows. Maybe he was upset that the honeymoon had been interrupted. Well, that was just tough luck. She shouldn't have been away in the first place, let alone doing what she had been doing.

But despite her sadness and worry Nena couldn't entirely banish the immediate undercurrent that flowed the instant she recalled last night. She glanced fleetingly at her husband, then turned away. It was wrong to feel like this when so much was at stake, with the end of her grandfather's life in the offing. Entirely wrong.

Ramon stood, impeccable as always in a well-tailored dark grey silk suit, leaning his arm on the corner of the mantelpiece. He carried on a stilted conversation with his mother, and watched as the butler brought in some tea and accepted a cup from him. He was aware that Nena just sat, looking numb, as though her world were crumbling about her. One look at Don Rodrigo and a quickly exchanged glance with his mother had been enough to tell him that the end was close at hand. Perhaps that was why they hadn't already taken him to hospital, he reflected sadly. Perhaps the old gentleman preferred to die at home in his own bed. And if that was the case then his wish should be respected.

He glanced over at Nena, seeing the determined line of her mouth. He must make her realise the truth. He could not allow her to drag her grandfather off, subject him to treatment that would do no good anyway just because of her need to keep him alive. At that moment Ramon understood that there was a lot more to marriage than just sleeping with his wife. The role of husband was also to help her take the right course of action. Nena and he might very well be up against their first hurdle, he realised with a flash of enlightenment.

For a minute he looked over at his mother, sitting gracefully near Nena, her silver hair perfectly coiffed, her Chanel suit worn with such elegance, and wondered what it could have been like for a young girl of eighteen to marry a man twenty years her elder, a man whom she'd barely known before the wedding, and asked himself if she'd ever regretted it. His parents certainly didn't ever give the impression of being unhappy. Quite the opposite, now he came to think of it. Perhaps there was something to be said for an arrangement of this sort after all.

The thought brought him up with a jolt.

God, he realised, horrified. In the flurry of the past few weeks he had completely forgotten to tell Luisa about the wedding and the changes in his life!

The sudden realisation left him raking his fingers savagely through his hair and wondering how on earth he was going to find a free moment to call her. How could he have been so thoughtless and remiss? He glanced over at Nena, realising, much to his surprise, that she had occupied his mind fully from the moment he'd first set eyes on her, and that since that day he'd barely thought about Luisa. But it would be discourteous and callous of him to allow the woman with whom he'd spent the better part of his leisure time over the past couple of years to learn of his nuptials in the press.

Strangely, his initial idea of maintaining Luisa on the side as his mistress seemed out of the question after last night. He shifted sideways and crossed one leg over the other. Merely recalling the previous evening's activities was causing an embarrassing change in his physical state.

Stop it, he ordered himself. *Stop acting like a teenager with a hormonal overdose.* He tried desperately to think of things that would dampen his ardour. But nothing sufficed to completely do the trick.

That night they stayed at Thurston Manor. Nena made it plain that they would be sleeping in separate bedrooms. Ramon was about to protest, then with a flash of insight realised that maybe she needed to be alone at this difficult time, and so he shut up.

Don Pedro had driven down from London to join them, and together they sat through a desultory dinner. No one was very hungry. Nena could barely eat a bite, her thoughts concentrated on her grandfather's room upstairs, where she'd spent the better part of the afternoon, sitting quietly in the chair next to the bed, stroking Don Rodrigo's frail white hand and praying that a miracle would occur to save him.

Despite her initial desire to sweep him off to hospital she had listened to her mother-in-law's words when Doña Augusta had gently suggested that perhaps her grandfather was happier where he was.

Later Ramon spoke to her in similar terms, and in spite of a profound desire to flout him—since she felt he was in a way responsible for her absence—and to whisk her grandfather onto a helicopter and off to hospital, she listened to the painful truth.

'Nena, I know how difficult this is for you to accept, but I think you must face the fact that the end may be close at hand,' Ramon said to her when they were alone in the hall. He made no attempt to take her hand or approach her, and stood several feet away.

'But he can't be that ill. There must be a solution,' she repeated for the hundredth time. 'Surely something can be done.'

'You heard the doctor, *querida*,' he said, gently but firmly. 'There is not much that can be done except keep him as comfortable as possible.'

At that Nena turned, her eyes full of tears, and ran up the stairs while he watched her, his bronzed hand fixed on the newel post, sensing that it was better to leave her be.

Again Ramon wanted to query the separate bedrooms issue. Not because he planned to have sex with her but because, he realised, he wanted to hold her—take her in his arms and give her the comfort he knew she so desperately needed. But, seeing how distant she'd become, he kept quiet. There would be time enough to console her once Don Rodrigo had passed on to a better world and when Nena realised the full truth of it. How wise the old gentleman had been to foresee the situation so clearly, he reflected. Soon it would be up to him to give his wife the kind of support she would need.

Still, the night alone would give him an opportunity to make the much needed phone call to Luisa, and once he was in his room Ramon braced himself, punched the quick-dial on his cellphone and waited while it rang over in Buenos Aires.

'Dígame.'

He heard Luisa's musical, throaty voice on the line and, surprisingly, did not experience the usual reaction.

'Lu, it's me,' he said automatically.

'Really, *querido?* And where might you be?'

'In England.'

'I see. If rumour has it right, you have been quite a busy boy of late.' Her voice was as icy as the waters of Antarctica.

'Look, Lu, I should have called you earlier, told you what was going on. But somehow I just didn't get around to it.' He closed his eyes and grimaced, imagining Luisa's livid face.

'So it's true,' she said, after a small hesitation.

'Yes, I'm afraid it is.'

'And you didn't even have the decency to call me and tell me personally?'

'I'm afraid I forgot.'

'You forgot. Well, Ramon, that is just wonderful. We spend two years having a white-hot affair, which has been splattered all over the press, and you simply "forget" to tell me that you're getting married. My congratulations,' she added frigidly.

'Lu, it's all my fault, I know, and I should have told you—of course I should. I could kick myself for not ringing you, but—'

'But what? Your child bride was taking up too much of your attention?' she asked sweetly.

'Don't be ridiculous. And she's not a child, she's—'

'Oh, shut up, Ramon. I don't even know why I'm talking to you. You deserve to be hung, drawn and quartered—and, believe me, if you were anywhere close by I'd do something a hell of a lot worse.'

Ramon shuddered, then smiled. 'Lu,' he said, his tone cajoling, 'you know that even though it's over between us I'll always adore you.'

'Hmm. Don't try and cajole me with your golden tongue, Ramon Villalba.' But she relented a little and laughed all the same. They were, after all, two of a kind—sophisticated jet-setters who knew the rules of the game and could remain friends.

The rest of the conversation was inconsequential and when it was over Ramon rang off, relieved. After reading a while he turned off the light to go to sleep.

He might have been considerably less at ease had he known that Nena, upon leaving her grandfather's room, had passed Ramon's closed door and overheard a single phrase that had left her running, anguished and furious with him and herself, to her own apartment.

I'll always adore you.

The words throbbed like cymbals in her ears. How could he? How could he make love to her, call her those endearing names one night, and the next be telling another woman that he would always adore her?

Nena threw off her dressing gown and climbed miserably into bed. This was the saddest, most awful time of her life. Her grandfather was no better and she was slowly coming to terms with the inevitable outcome. And now just as she'd been telling herself that perhaps there was something to be said for his insistence that she marry and not be left out in the world all on her own, she had overheard those dreadful words.

Well, she consoled herself, huddling under the covers and blowing her nose determinedly, it was probably better to know the truth and not make a complete fool of herself again, as she had the previous night.

But that was it.

From now on she would insist they sleep separately. Ramon was obviously a very talented actor. But now she had been well and thoroughly alerted. And, she reflected, throwing a pillow furiously out of the bed, she would do well to heed the warning that inadvertently she'd been privileged to overhear.

CHAPTER FOUR

THREE days later, at three thirty-eight a.m., Don Rodrigo passed away. Nena, who had barely left his side for the past seventy-two hours, finally collapsed from emotional exhaustion and, laying her head on her grandfather's still chest, cried her heart out. It wasn't just losing him, but also all that had changed, all that would change for ever in her life. In the space of three weeks she'd been thrown into a tailspin, and now her one point of gravity, her grandfather, was gone.

It was thus that Ramon found her when he came quietly into the room two hours later.

'Nena—oh, my God,' he muttered, hurrying to her side and laying his hand on her head to stroke her hair. 'I'm so sorry, *amor mio,* so dreadfully sorry.'

After several minutes he forced her to sit up, to move her stiff limbs, to take her eyes off the wax-like figure lying motionless in the bed.

The nurse, who had tactfully remained out of sight until the moment was over and Nena had said her final goodbye to her grandfather, came forward. Ramon, his arm firmly gripping her shoulders, shepherded her from the room.

'You must rest,' he insisted, guiding her in the direction of her bedroom. Then, seeing that she could barely walk from exhaustion, he scooped her into his arms and carried her, as he would a child, then deposited her gently onto the bed.

'Now let me cover you,' he murmured, pulling back the covers and sliding her legs under them before tucking her in and sitting on the edge of the bed. Her eyes seemed vacant, her limbs numb. But he knew that for now all he could do was try and soothe her to sleep.

Nena's eyes closed, and after several minutes she glided into an exhausted sleep. Somewhere through the haze of her mind and soul the gentle movement of Ramon's fingers massaging her neck and stroking her hair reached her. But it barely registered. Only when she woke several hours later and found him still seated next to her, dressed, his hand on her shoulder, having fallen asleep against the pillows, did she become fully aware of his presence.

Nena sat up, careful not to wake him. Despite her antipathy, and her anger at the words she'd heard him say the other night, she could not help but be touched by this unselfish display of solidarity. A rush of sudden affection swept over her and gently she tried to accommodate him better.

Ramon shifted towards the centre of the bed and instinctively pulled his legs up onto it. Then, as naturally as though they'd been sleeping together for years, he flung an arm across her and drew her close, murmuring something indistinguishable in his sleep.

For a moment Nena held her breath and lay stiffly, a prisoner in his grip, unwilling to wake him. Then, hearing the regular breathing and certain he really was asleep, she slowly relaxed, closed her eyes once more, and willed reality to stay away for as long as possible.

She felt strangely warm and protected in her husband's arms. Maybe he had told another woman he adored her, and maybe this was all fake, she conceded, but right now—just at this crucial moment—she needed the human companionship and warmth that he was offering, albeit in sleep.

At ten o'clock Doña Augusta decided to check on Nena. Peeping round the door she was surprised to see her lying in her son's embrace. Both were fast asleep. Her face broke into a soft smile, lessening some of the tension of the past few hours. Then gently she closed the door behind her and descended the stairs to find her husband.

There was so much to be attended to—funeral arrangements, the gathering afterwards. Nena was incapable of handling such responsibilities in her present state, and with the natural grace of habit Doña Augusta took over. The relieved servants turned to her for their instructions, instinctively bowing to her well-bred automatic sense of command, glad to delegate responsibility.

And so it was that when Nena and Ramon finally woke and blinked into each other's eyes, downstairs nothing had been left to chance.

As soon as she became conscious of her situation Nena wriggled and tried to escape.

'Don't go,' Ramon said, pulling a hand through his tousled hair. 'You're too tired to get up. You need to rest, Nena.'

'I have to get up. There is so much to do—so much to take care of. Grandfather would have expected me to be on board, whatever my feelings,' she answered, feeling her limbs stiff with tension and trying to stretch.

'Here, let me give you a massage.' Not waiting for an answer, Ramon turned her peremptorily on her tummy and began kneading her shoulders.

'I—'

'Shut up and relax,' he commanded in an authoritative tone. 'You'll be no good to anyone if you're all wound up. And, as you said, there is much to be dealt with.'

Too tired to argue, Nena gave way, experiencing a thrill as her muscles began to relax. She closed her eyes and let him work on her back, down and down, unable to do more than let out the odd sigh from time to time, exhale and allow the tension to dissipate as his hands pressed exactly the right pressure points, the ones that were aching. Then all at once the massaging turned to caressing, and still she didn't move. When his hands slipped from her lower back to her bottom she lay totally still, allowing him to follow the rounded curves without protest.

Slowly Ramon slipped his hand under her nightdress, stroking her thighs lightly, relaxing them, unable to resist the temptation or the powerful tug that drew him to this woman, to her body, her mind and soul. He needed to enter her, feel her, to let her know that she was not alone, that he was here for her, to cherish and protect her, to help expedite the pain. Wasn't that, after all, what he had promised to do?

His hand reached further, until he parted her thighs and let his thumb roam, and a thrill of delight coursed through him when he felt the delicious wetness that told him more than words could just how much she needed him. Leaning over, he kissed the back of her neck and stroked her intimately, hearing the tiny moan, feeling her buttocks arch up to meet him.

Nena let out a long sigh. Part of her protested inwardly while another craved more. And she could do no more than submit to his caresses. Then, when she let out an involuntary cry of pleasure and relived once more that same wonderful release she'd experienced several days earlier, Ramon turned her around.

She saw the raw passion written in his eyes and gasped, felt him all but tear her nightgown from her, then arched back as he thrust deep within her, joining him in a tempestuous encounter, perfectly rhymed, an intuitive dance of which both seemed to know the steps. He was gripping her small waist, pulling down on her hips, delving into her core, as though determined to drive away sorrow, death and the anguish of the previous hours, to let life take hold. Then once again they crashed together in that rollicking surf before falling, embracing among the sheets and into another much needed bout of sleep.

'I think we should return to Buenos Aires,' Ramon said several days later.

'But I don't think that's a good idea at all,' Nena protested, thinking suddenly of the woman whom he'd told he adored. Surely she must be there in Buenos Aires, waiting for him? Maybe, she reflected bitterly, that was why he was in such a hurry to go.

It was a lowering thought that made her remember all too clearly the lovemaking of the past days. Ramon had not left her bed again, had insisted they sleep together, and because she was too overwhelmed by the events going on about her, and because—although she hated to admit it—the feel of his arms about her was so wonderfully comforting, and his body next to and inside hers was so incredibly reassuring, she'd conceded.

Now the truth came ramming home and she sat bolt upright in her chair and looked at the floor.

'Why don't you go to Buenos Aires, Ramon? I have nothing to do there. Plus, I need to wrap up so many things here—see people, take care of some of Grandfather's affairs. I wasn't able to talk to many of his friends at the funeral, and I need to write thank-you notes and—'

'Nena, that's ridiculous and you know it. We met with all your grandfather's legal advisors yesterday. And I will be dealing with the Carvajal interests from now on, you know that. As for thank-you notes— well, we have perfectly good writing paper in BA.'

'I don't see why we have to go,' she said stubbornly, the thought of going back to Argentina clouded by all she knew awaited him there—principally Luisa, too much to handle.

'I would have thought it was obvious,' he answered firmly. 'I have my companies to deal with, my *hacienda*. My businesses to run as well as yours,' he added with a touch of humour. 'Why are you so reluctant to go?'

For a brief moment she nearly told him about the magazine and the article she'd read. Then dignity and pride got the better of her, and, tossing her tawny head, she looked straight at him.

'I don't think it's the right time.'

'Quite the contrary. You know it has to happen some time. Much better to go now, let all this settle. You need a break—to get away and relax after all the strain.'

'I hardly think BA will be relaxing,' she murmured witheringly.

'I don't see why not. It's a very pleasant part of the world. You'll make friends, have a life there as well as in London and Paris and all the other places we live. But it is, after all, going to be our main home. I want to buy a new house or an apartment.'

'Oh? What's wrong with the one you've got?' she enquired, eyes challenging.

'Nothing. But it's more of a bachelor's pad than anything else. Far too small for a family.'

'We're only two people,' she said, raising a brow. 'And who knows? I might just like it.'

'No,' he said firmly, and she saw a flicker of determination in his eyes. 'We'll stay in a suite at the Alvear until we find something that suits us.'

Nena did not argue. She had realised by now that when Ramon made up his mind about something there was little use fighting it. He didn't shout or bark or lose his temper, he merely used a quiet, very commanding tone of voice that allowed the listener no doubt as to the outcome of the matter.

Well, so be it, she reflected, with a sigh. In a way maybe it *was* better to get going. One day she would have to face the truth, and perhaps the sooner she did—came out of this fantasy world she'd been living in for the past few weeks—the better it would be. She must face life alone, she realised sadly, watching his turned back with a pang of sadness and something more. It was hard to know that he could be so passionate in bed with her and be just as powerful and giving with another woman.

The thought hurt, and Nena turned, gazing fiercely towards the window, determined that he shouldn't see her anguish. She'd deal with it—get it under control, rid herself of this stupid jealousy she was experiencing as the picture in the magazine flashed before her once more.

And in the end she'd win.

Ever since she was a child it had always struck Nena as strange to leave London in midsummer and arrive in Buenos Aires with a heavy coat on her arm.

Now they had arrived at the Alvear Palace, the *grande dame* of hotels in Buenos Aires, and some of her initial qualms were appeased. Ramon was attentive and thoughtful, making sure she was not relegated to second place, as had been her fear, but very much in the limelight.

Still grieving for her grandfather, Nena didn't feel like any social activities. But Ramon insisted he take her out on their first evening, to an amusing restaurant on the Ricoletta. They would eat wonderful *assados,* composed of fabulous Argentinian meat, and maybe watch the tango danced at the Viejo Almazen.

And then he came up with a complete surprise that, despite her efforts to regard him in an uncompromising light, touched her heart just the same.

They were at dinner, and reaching the pudding stage, when suddenly Ramon leaned across the table.

'Nena, *mi linda,*' he said, his voice low, his eyes penetrating, 'I owe you.'

'Owe me?' She frowned, not understanding. 'You don't owe me anything that I can think of.' Actually, if she were truthful, she probably owed him. Ramon had taken charge of her grandfather's affairs in a forceful and efficient manner that had left the advisors and trustees in no doubt as to who was in charge.

'Oh, but I do,' he insisted. At the same time he removed two small leather boxes from his jacket pocket. 'This is the first thing I owe you.' He slid a red Cartier box across the table.

Nena hesitated, her pulse beating suddenly faster. Then tentatively she opened the box. A beautiful diamond ring sparkled up at her. Ramon reached across and removed it from its velvet bed. Smiling at Nena, he lifted her left hand and slipped the ring onto her finger, next to her wedding band. 'That,' he said, eyes gazing straight into hers, 'is your engagement ring. If you don't like it we can have it changed.'

'Oh, no, I love it. It's perfectly lovely,' she assured him, gazing down at the perfect jewel, touched that he'd taken the trouble to remember such a detail.

'And this,' he said, opening a long thin jewel box, 'is your wedding present.' He removed a glistening, delicately woven diamond and sapphire bracelet.

Nena held up her wrist, enchanted. 'It's perfectly gorgeous, Ramon. It's vintage, isn't it?' she exclaimed, eyeing the bracelet and biting her lip, unable to express just how much the gesture meant.

'Yes. I saw it in a catalogue for a Sotheby's sale and had my man in Paris bid for it. I know you probably inherited masses of vintage jewellery from your mother and grandmother, but this struck me as a rather special piece.'

'Oh, it is!' she exclaimed, fighting back the tears that welled in her eyes. She felt suddenly bad. For here she was, trying to reject this man, when he was making every effort to make a success of their marriage. Perhaps she was being very silly and immature. She looked up at him and smiled tenderly across the table. 'Thank you, Ramon, I'm very touched. It was lovely to think of this.'

'It's the least I owe you,' he said gruffly. Then, taking her hand, he turned it around and kissed the inside of her wrist, sending delicious shudders up her arm and reminding her that the evening was not entirely over. She had been reticent near him since their arrival in BA, afraid that Luisa might be just around the corner.

But now he'd dispelled most of her fears. Here, in the quiet, well-attended restaurant, with its sophisticated décor and discreet waiters, she felt suddenly very, very happy—glad that she was here with him and not back in England, mourning her beloved grandfather all on her own.

They decided to walk down the wide avenues back to the hotel. Nena had vague memories of taking tea there with her grandparents and her mother and father when she must have been a very little girl.

'I can still just recall coming here with my mother,' she told Ramon as they stepped into the lobby. 'Do they still have English afternoon tea with scones?' she asked, with a touch of nostalgia for her mother, the woman who had flitted so briefly through her life.

'Of course. The Alvear never loses its touch or its old traditions. I can see that it must have been very hard for you, growing up with no parents,' he added, glancing at her and securing her arm more firmly in his.

'In a way, but then I had my grandparents. They were wonderful to me.'

'When did your grandmother die?'

'Four years ago. Grandfather never got over her

death. He was never quite the same after that. They loved one another so much.'

'Yet they had an arranged marriage?' he said thoughtfully.

'Yes. And so, apparently, did your parents. They seem very happy too. They've been so kind to me.'

'So they should—they've just acquired a daughter.'

'Is that really how they feel?' she asked, turning and looking up at him. 'Or are you just saying that to make me feel better about all this?'

'No. I really mean it. My mother adores you and my father's half in love with you himself.'

She giggled as they tripped up the steps and through the blue-carpeted lobby to the elevator, then on up to their suite.

'Tomorrow we're meeting with the estate agents,' Ramon said as they reached their door. 'They have a number of houses and apartments to show us. Which do you think you'd prefer?' he asked casually as they entered the drawing room of the suite, taking off his jacket and slinging it over the back of a chair while Nena hung up her coat in the cupboard.

'What? You mean a house or an apartment?' she asked, tilting her head. 'I really don't know. I—you see, I never thought of getting a house of my—our— own so soon. It's all rather a novelty.'

'Good. We'll have fun choosing then,' he said, sitting down on the sofa. 'I don't suppose you want to watch TV, do you?'

'Why not? Let's see what's on.' She sent him a dazzling smile and curled next to him on the sofa as if they'd been doing this for aeons. It felt good. It felt natural. And Nena sensed a chill of fear at just how used she was getting to sharing her life with this man whom she barely knew.

Ramon flipped the remote control. 'Oh, Lord. Look—it's the Britcoms. *Fawlty Towers* and Manuel!'

'Oh, please, leave it on!' she exclaimed, touching his arm. 'It's so funny.'

'I doubt there's anything much else on, except CNN and the news,' he answered, leaning back and slipping his arm around her while laughing at one of John Cleese's inimitable gestures.

An hour later they were both doubled over with laughter, relaxed and enjoying every minute of the evening. Nena had kicked off her shoes and Ramon had his feet up on the ottoman, ankles crossed.

It had been a perfect evening, she reflected, glancing down at her wrist and her finger. All the fears she'd had about coming here were suddenly obliterated by his gesture and the manner in which he'd managed to set her at ease. She felt excited now about choosing their new home, and imagined what it might be like, thought of how she would decorate it. Doña Augusta would have to help her get to know the various shops and decorators when she returned from London.

'Okay, sleepyhead,' he said, ruffling her hair and dropping a kiss on her brow, 'Time for bed, I think. We have quite a day tomorrow.'

Nena smiled, smothered a yawn, stretched and let him pull her up from the sofa. Then all at once there was an imperceptible change in the atmosphere. Their eyes locked and in one swift movement Ramon pressed her hard against him.

'I want you,' he growled, slipping his hands on her

bottom and pressing her against him, letting her feel his hardness.

'And I want you,' she whispered back, gazing up at him, feeling herself go completely liquid inside.

'Then what are we waiting for?'

In one quick gesture Ramon unzipped her dress. It fell in a circle about her feet. Then he flicked open her bra hook and flipped it aside. 'My beautiful, gorgeous *señora*,' he muttered, cupping her breasts and grazing her nipples with his thumb, causing her to draw in her breath as she worked desperately on the buttons of his shirt and the buckle of his belt.

Minutes later they were lying naked in the huge Empire bed, Ramon's tongue working magic on her. But this time Nena wanted to adventure herself, and when he lifted his head she pushed him back on the bed.

Ramon quirked a surprised eyebrow, then, seeing her determined expression, gave way as she tentatively began kissing his throat, his chest, and down, down, until her lips closed falteringly around him.

She heard him draw in his breath.

'*Mi amor,*' he muttered, huskily surprised.

That was all the encouragement she needed. Soon they were writhing together, kissing, biting. Ramon thrust deep within her, possessing every inch of her, and she possessed him.

And Nena knew a new and powerful satisfaction: that of having truly pleased her man.

At ten o'clock the estate agent picked them up in a smart four-wheel drive to visit several addresses on his list. The first two were not suitable, and were immediately discarded, the third was a lovely house, but had a garden that needed a complete overhaul, but the fourth, a thousand-square-metre penthouse in an attractive building in the upmarket district of Palermo, enchanted them.

'What a magnificient view!' Nena exclaimed, gazing out over the city. 'It looks so like Paris, doesn't it?'

'Yes, it does. Do you like this place, Nena?'

'Yes. I think it's wonderful.'

'Nice ample bedroom,' Ramon muttered, out of earshot of the agent.

'Hmm,' she murmured, trying not to giggle and digging her elbow into his ribs to keep him quiet.

'And room for a nursery,' he added, slipping his arm about her as they walked out onto the wide wraparound balcony.

'I don't plan on having kids for a long time,' Nena pronounced briskly.

'No, of course not.' He nodded blandly. 'Still, it's good not to have to move too often, don't you think?'

'Absolutely,' she agreed. 'Much more practical.'

'Shall we take it, then?'

'Yes,' she said, her face lighting up with a radiant smile that left him wanting to return immediately to the hotel.

It was quite amazing, he reflected as he went back inside the living room to discuss the terms with the agent, just how Nena had captured his whole being. And, if he was really truthful, he realised ruefully, his heart. He had never experienced such tenderness for a woman, such a feeling of warmth, such an intense need to be with her, return to her when they were separated even for a few hours.

Was this what marriage was all about?

*　　*　　*

Two days later Ramon called Nena on her cellphone.

'*Mi amor,* I have to go to the *hacienda* for a few days. A problem has cropped up that I must deal with personally.'

'Oh. Shall I come with you?'

'No. I don't think it's worth it. I'll have to be on the go the whole time. I want to be able to spend time with you the first time you go there.'

'All right. I can get going with the apartment, then. I have a few addresses. Your cousin Pablo's wife, Elisa, kindly said she'd take me to several decorating establishments.'

'Good. She's a great girl. I'm glad you've made a friend.'

'When will you be flying out?' Nena asked, the thought of him being away leaving her lonely.

'Early tomorrow morning. Don't worry, *cariña,* we still have tonight,' he murmured, leaving her blushing at the feelings his words evoked.

The next day Nena met Elisa to go shopping, and then continued with her on for lunch at Santi's, a trendy lunch spot in the Ricoletta. They were seated at a corner table which offered them a full view of the busy restaurant.

It was obviously the 'in' place for ladies' lunches, Nena realised, watching a positive catwalk of the latest fashions, worn by rake-thin, angular, good-looking Argentine women who walked by with a self-assured, slightly arrogant air, as though they owned the world.

Nena ordered a salad, and Elisa a thin entrecôte.

'I'm dieting—low carbs,' she said, grinning.

'But you're so thin already.'

'Must keep it up, darling. You're young, but I'm hitting thirty. Positively ancient. Have to preserve my figure.'

Nena laughed and shook her head. Everyone here seemed so conscious of the way they looked and dressed and projected themselves. It made her feel rather young and unsophisticated, despite her exposure to London and Paris. It was just a different way of life where the physical was more interwoven into the general consciousness.

'Ah, there's Ana and Mariella over there,' Elisa said, waving to two friends. 'I must introduce them to you. You'll like them. They're great fun.'

It was just as the waiter was laying their espressos on the table that Nena looked up and, to her amazement, recognised the woman standing at a nearby table, chatting. She shuddered, certain it was the woman she'd seen pictured in *Hola!* magazine. And not ten feet away. She caught her breath and swallowed a gasp. Of course this would have happened some day, she supposed. She just wished it hadn't been when her husband was away.

'Do you know her?' Elisa asked curiously, seeing Nena's gaze fixed on Luisa.

'Oh, no. But she's very good-looking, isn't she?'

'Yes,' Elisa responded warily, 'she is. Very.'

Nena took a sidelong glance at Elisa and caught the troubled expression in her eyes.

'Don't worry,' she said, trying to sound nonchalant and very grown-up, 'I know all about her and Ramon.'

'You do?' Elisa looked surprised.

'Yes. It doesn't bother me,' she lied with a shrug.

'That's very sensible of you,' Elisa responded approvingly. 'Much better to be realistic about these things.'

Nena didn't add that she felt confident that now that she and Ramon were spending every day together and every night passionately making love his affair with Luisa must be over.

The woman turned and sent a long glance in her direction, then leaned forward and murmured something to the woman she was sitting down next to, who in turn murmured to her neighbour. Suddenly they were all looking at her critically, and Nena felt herself blushing despite her determination to carry on as if nothing untoward had taken place.

'Pay no attention to them,' Elisa said, waving blithely at Luisa and her table. 'They don't mean any harm; they're just curious about you. After all, Ramon is a very big catch. Luisa and he had been going together for a couple of years, and frankly the whole thing must have come as a great shock to her.'

'Naturally. It must have,' Nena agreed, suddenly seeing the flipside of the coin. It must have been very difficult for Luisa to be ousted from one day to the next. For a moment she felt sorry for the older woman. Other people's feelings had no place in their arranged marriage, and she wondered suddenly if Ramon had really broken off with Luisa after all.

A niggling doubt assailed her as she recalled the night at Thurston Manor when she'd passed Ramon's door and heard him say *I'll always adore you.* Had it been Luisa he'd been talking to?

She glanced furtively in the other woman's direction, not wanting to be obvious. Luisa looked proud and beautifully groomed. Her long, glistening dark hair hung straight on the shoulders of her white cashmere jersey, she wore suede pants and high-heeled boots and looked sure of every inch of herself, Nena reflected. Would a woman who'd just been abandoned by a man like Ramon, with whom she'd had such a public affair, be flaunting herself like this in a restaurant? Laughing, elbows lightly poised on the table, her perfectly manicured fingers with their sparkling diamonds elegantly clasped, chattering as though she hadn't a worry in the world?

Perhaps it was just an act, and inside she was suffering, but the woman's exuberance and self-confidence left Nena feeling a little—not dowdy, exactly—but not quite up to par.

'Let's go clothes-shopping this afternoon,' she said suddenly to her companion. 'I'd like to buy some of the wonderful suede things they have here—some pants, skirts and things.'

'Why, of course,' Elisa said, smiling, brushing her pretty brown hair back from her attractive tanned face. 'I'll take you to my favourite boutique right now.'

Nena felt relieved when they exited the restaurant and she was finally free of the prying eyes she'd felt following her.

As the afternoon flew by and they visited various shops and boutiques the uncomfortable, uneasy feeling that had gripped her gradually wore off, and by the time she reached the Alvear, loaded with huge shopping bags, she felt back to her old self again.

Ramon exited the company plane in Cordoba, where his manager was waiting to drive him to the *hacienda*. But first he had a meeting scheduled with the governor of the province, and a few banking details to be dealt with.

However, by four p.m. he was saddled up and galloping over the pampas, inspecting his cattle, his mind busy with the details that needed to be attended to.

Then finally, as he turned his horse around and began cantering back towards the *hacienda,* he had time to reflect upon all that had taken place over the past few weeks—how his life had made a three-hundred-and-sixty-degree turn and how strangely happy he felt in this new existence. The only thing that bothered him was his unforgivable behaviour towards Luisa. After all, she must have learned that he was back in town by now, somebody would have made sure to tell her, and she must be wondering why he hadn't been in touch.

In fact, he rather wondered himself.

Okay, he'd been taken up with showing Nena around, finding the apartment and one thing and another, but still it did not explain his reluctance to face Luisa and have the final conversation he knew he owed her, which would have to take place at some time or another in the near future.

He sighed and slowed to a trot. Perhaps the best thing would be to stop off and see her on his way back to town. That way he wouldn't be obliged to lie to his wife—wouldn't have to mix apples and pears. Somehow it was important that the fragile confidence he'd established with Nena endured. The last thing he needed was to have his mistress—ex-mistress, he reminded himself quickly—thrust upon her at any given moment.

Seeing Luisa for the last time and getting the whole thing straightened out, he decided, returning to the stables, was definitely the right way to manage this whole affair.

Satisfied that he'd found the correct solution, Ramon dismounted and walked slowly back to the lovely colonial farmhouse that had been in his family for several generations, since the King of Spain had given his ancestor these tracts of land. He looked forward to bringing Nena here, showing her the place and letting her get her hands wet redecorating. The place certainly needed it. His mother very rarely came to Santa Clara any more, finding the climate too rude, but he had the feeling Nena would enjoy riding in the pampas and sharing this place with him—something he had never done with any other woman before, he mused. This had always been his private enclave. Now, to his utter surprise, he had no qualms about sharing it.

CHAPTER FIVE

'I KNOW I should have told you,' Ramon repeated, looking over at Luisa sitting opposite him on an ultra-modern sofa in her exquisitely decorated apartment that he knew so well. 'I am entirely to blame in this whole affair, Luisa.'

'So you keep saying,' Luisa replied, eyeing him askance and wondering, now that they were face to face, if there might not be a way of hanging on to him despite his marriage to the girl she'd seen the other day at Santi's. Okay, his new wife was young and lovely. But wouldn't that youth and lack of experience bore him after a little? And, when the novelty wore off, wouldn't he prefer to take a break in her arms once in a while?

Luisa thought it over warily. She must be careful not to push him. She knew Ramon well enough to recognise that stubborn twitch around his lips, knew that when he was committed to something he went for it full throttle. Still, handled with kid gloves, there was no saying what might happen. She might just be able to revert this situation in her favour. Of course, it would never be quite the same again—but what in life was?

She sighed inwardly. She had strong feelings for

Ramon, and was not disposed, she realised suddenly, to just let him disappear out of her life without so much as a by-your-leave. At first she'd been furiously angry, insulted and hurt. Now the hurt remained, but common sense prevailed.

'I'm famished!' she exclaimed, stretching and reaching over to touch his arm. 'Why don't we go and have a bite in one of our special haunts, for old times' sake?' She smiled at him winningly.

Ramon had little desire to be seen publicly in Luisa's company, but to refuse the invitation after she'd been such a good sport—had taken the rejection in such a well-spirited manner—would be churlish.

'Okay,' he agreed, disguising his reluctance as he rose. 'I'm afraid I can't stay too late, though.'

'Of course not,' she said in a cajoling tone, while slipping her smooth bronzed arm through his and letting him get a whiff of her perfume. 'You're a married man now, and you have obligations after all.'

'Uh, yes.' He laughed uncomfortably while Luisa made sure that her thigh rubbed gently against his as they moved towards the hall to slip on their jackets.

'Let's go to Santi's. It should be pretty quiet on a Thursday at lunchtime,' she proposed, tossing her large leather handbag over her shoulder.

'Fine. Great idea,' he replied, all in favour of a place that would not be jampacked with half their friends and acquaintances.

But Luisa's prognostication proved to be wrong. Santi's was, in fact, filled with just the kind of people Ramon had hoped to avoid, and it took them a full ten minutes to get from the door to their table, there were so many friends to greet.

'Hi, Ramon, good to see you back in town. Let's get together.'

The greetings were endless, and the curious looks and interested murmurs that followed them in no way suppressed.

Luisa smothered a grin of satisfaction. Her plan had worked after all. She pretended to pay no attention to the disturbance they were causing, to the chattering couples all speculating as to what was going on in Ramon's life. Well, let them. The more the merrier, Luisa decided as she studied her menu.

Ramon sat silently furious, but could do nothing without causing a scene. He could see now what Luisa's game was, and was thoroughly annoyed with himself for having fallen for it. Well, let the games begin, he decided, calmly ordering his favourite dish. 'Oh, and don't forget the *chimi churri* sauce, will you?' he said to the waiter, with a grin that belied his inner anger.

He thought of Nena. He'd told her he would be back today but didn't know what time. Was she back at the hotel waiting for him? he wondered impatiently. God, Luisa could be a bitch when she set her mind to it. And somehow now all her faults glared straight at him. How come, he wondered, carrying on a light-hearted and amusing conversation with her, hadn't he recognised them clearly before?

'Oh, he won't be back until late,' Elisa assured Nena as they left the boutique where Nena had had to pick up several articles of suede clothing she'd ordered. 'Let's have a bite of lunch, and afterwards I can drop you off at the Alvear on my way home.'

'Okay, sounds good,' Nena responded with a smile.

She felt good in a new pair of trousers, a smart polo-neck cashmere top, a suede vest bordered with fur, and a very smart pair of Chanel sunglasses that set off her glistening well-trimmed hair, swinging around her shoulders. She had been to Carlos, Elisa's top-of-the-line hairdresser, and felt more a part of the elegant lifestyle of the women in this sophisticated city. She found it fun and amusing. And, although her grandfather was never far from her mind, her propulsion into this entirely different new existence had done wonders to help overcome her initial sadness.

But she missed Ramon.

It was extraordinary to think that only a month or so ago she hadn't even known the man who had made such a mark upon her being, and without whom she now found it difficult to imagine life.

'Santi's, as usual?' Elisa asked with a grin.

She liked Nena very much, was thrilled that Ramon had finally—through no merit of his own—fallen on someone so perfect for him, and had enthusiastically taken Nena under her wing, introducing her to friends and showing her the ropes. But she knew that of all the places she'd taken the girl, the fashionable and trendy Santi's was her favourite.

'If you don't mind going there again, I'd love to,' Nena replied, laughing. 'It's always such fun. And I love their *empanados*.'

'I just hope that Franco will be able to give us a

decent table. If worse comes to worst we can have a glass of champagne or something at the bar while we wait.'

But when they entered the packed restaurant Franco had no hesitation in finding them a small table for two tucked in a corner that had just been vacated, and the girls wound their way among the busy tables. Nena even had a few people to say hello to herself now, and everyone seemed pleased to see her.

It was Elisa who first caught the furtive glances directed upwards, towards the elevated gallery. That and the overly bright smiles. She frowned, her radar immediately picking up the silent messages being sent her way. But it was too late. Nena looked up too soon.

Words could not describe the chill, the utter horror she experienced when she saw them—the woman, Luisa, from the magazine, leaning towards Ramon touching his cheek in a manner denoting complete intimacy and familiarity.

At first Nena could hardly move as indescribable pain seared through her. Then, as though by some miracle of will, she reacted, pulled herself together in the space of a few seconds and went on talking as though nothing untoward had happened. But it seemed hours until they reached the table, where she sat on the edge of the bench, barely able to breathe.

'What's the matter, Nena? You look pale,' Elisa said with a worried frown.

'I'm fine.' She sent the other woman a bright, brittle smile and tossed her hair back elegantly, damned if she was going to make a complete idiot of herself. She'd been a fool to think Ramon would give up his old lifestyle so easily, that just because he spent so much time in her bed he'd forsake his mistress. Stupid and naïve were the correct terms. Why, oh, why hadn't she followed her initial instinct and kept the marriage as it had been initially conceived? An arrangement. A satisfactory solution to a problem. But, no. She'd allowed herself to be swept off her feet, to fall victim to his immense charm, to his delightful manners, falling prey to his demonstrations of kindness and, let's face it, to the passion and intimacy he'd taught her and that now formed an integral part of her existence.

Foolish and unprepared. That was what she was. Perhaps it had amused Ramon to teach her a few things, men liked to be the first man in a woman's life, to show her the ropes, she reflected cynically, determined not to peek up towards the gallery but to maintain her dignity. She'd thought he too was enjoying their being together. Ha! What a stupid illusion. In point of fact where he really enjoyed himself was with the sophisticated Luisa, a woman of the world, one with whom he shared similar interests, friends and a life. All she was, Nena realised suddenly, swallowing back the tears welling inside and determined not to give way, was a fish out of water.

Not now.

She would not, she vowed, *could* not make a spectacle of herself in public. Whatever it cost, she would hold it together, eat the food that was put before her and carry on a normal, civilised conversation with Elisa as if nothing had happened. She would not, she assured herself, give that woman up there the pleasure of seeing her defeated.

Uneasily, Elisa glanced towards the gallery. She wondered if Nena had seen the couple and hesitated, caught between her desire to warn the girl and her doubt as to whether she'd noticed them. Better not mention it, she decided, in case she hadn't. But the girl looked so pale, so drawn. And despite her efforts to make conversation and appear at ease Elisa could tell something was wrong.

She must have seen them, Elisa figured, her heart going out to Ramon's young wife, admiring her dignity and her pride, and the fact that she hadn't made a scene or rushed from the restaurant in tears. It took guts to face up to something like this, and she was pleased to see that Nena was no lightweight. In fact, she reflected, taking a quick peek at Ramon, apparently engrossed in conversation with Luisa, she sincerely hoped that Nena would give him a run for his money. It would do him no harm at all.

Okay, many men had double lives. The story of the *casa grande* and the *casa pequeña* was all too common—it was almost a status thing for a man to keep a beautiful mistress. But somehow Elisa felt this situation was different. There was a streak of determination in Nena that was not to be messed with. And she would not be the least surprised, Elisa reflected, if in the end Nena didn't win the day.

Ramon rose from the table and moved aside for Luisa to pass ahead of him. Again she made sure her thigh grazed his, then turned back and spoke to him in an intimate manner as they descended the few steps from the gallery to the main part of the restaurant, touching his arm possessively.

It was at that precise moment that he saw Nena, seated at a table straight in their passage.

'*Madre de Dios,*' he muttered under his breath.

Luisa walked ahead, smiling at their friends, stopping from time to time, making sure the whole place saw them together. He could throttle her! How had he allowed himself to be sucked into this? Should he talk to Nena or pretend he hadn't seen her? From all he could see she appeared to be having an animated conversation with his cousin's wife Elisa.

But there was no way he could avoid direct contact with their table. Allowing Luisa to walk on ahead, heart sinking, he approached the two women, aware that every eye in the restaurant was fixed upon him. He knew the crowd only too well—knew all the restaurant was waiting in titillating suspense to see what he'd do. For a moment he hesitated. Then he made up his mind.

Damn Luisa and her below-the-belt tricks! His wife was more important, he realised suddenly, aching for her, admiring the way she was pretending to be oblivious of the scene when she must have seen him.

'*Hola,*' he said, dropping a hand on Elisa's shoulder and a kiss on the top of her head. His eyes met Nena's glittering ones across the table. 'Nena. I—'

'Hello, Ramon.' She sent him a brittle smile that cost her a fortune in will-power. She wished she could get up right there and send a ringing slap onto that bronzed cheek of his. Instead she posed her hands elegantly on the table. 'What a coincidence that we should find ourselves in the same restaurant. I thought you were returning later in the day.'

'I was,' he muttered. 'When will you be back at the hotel?' he asked curtly.

'I have no idea,' she responded coldly. 'Oh, look, you'd better run along. Your friend is waiting at the door.'

'Very well,' he agreed stiffly. 'I'll see you at the Alvear later.'

Nena gave him a nod and a smile for the benefit of the crowd, pretending not to stare. She had never been so humiliated in the entire course of her short existence, and once, she vowed, rage stirring in her as never before, was enough.

'Bravo, Nena,' Elisa whispered fervently across the table once Ramon had disappeared. 'You were simply terrific. I can't admire you enough for the way you behaved. Luisa must have brought him here to try and prove to people that they are still together.'

'Well, she was just proving the truth by the looks of it, wasn't she?' Nena responded, the neutral tone of her voice belying her boiling inner turmoil. She could kill the man, quite literally strangle him for the pain she was feeling, the utter humiliation and sheer anguish of seeing him so intimately next to another woman.

And Luisa in particular.

She would tear Luisa's eyes out too, if she got half a chance, she realised, a sudden new emotion that she recognised as jealousy searing though her like a white-hot arrow.

As they silently returned to the hotel Nena's mind was on fire. She wondered when Ramon would make his appearance. If he would be there when she walked in, or if he would only come back later. But what did it really matter? She had no intention of staying anyway.

After thanking Elisa for her kindness and saying goodbye, Nena went hurriedly up to the suite and, hand trembling unlocked the door.

There was no sign of Ramon, she realised, relieved, throwing her shopping bags onto the bed and heading straight for the closet, where she dragged out her two large suitcases.

Then turning around she picked up the phone.

'Ah, concierge? Yes. I'd like you to book me a place on the British Airways flight to London tonight, please. Yes, first class. By the window. Thank you.'

She laid down the receiver and swallowed. She'd been foolish to follow him here, to do his bidding, but it was still not too late to remedy matters.

Determined not to give way to her pent-up rage, Nena folded each item of clothing carefully before inserting it in the case. She would not allow him the satisfaction of seeing her fall apart—would not let him know how deeply he'd affected her feelings, how much the past few days and weeks had come to mean to her. They obviously represented very little to him, so what was the point?

Half an hour later she was packed and ready to leave. She called for a bellboy, still mustering all her control. The tears that had been fighting their way to the fore would just have to wait until she was by herself. Well away from him and this place.

Ramon drove furiously back to the hotel. His leave-taking from Luisa had been cold and angry. She'd set him up, and for that he would never forgive her. Maybe she hadn't known Nena would actually be in the restaurant—that was simply an added bonus—but she must have calculated that it would be jam-packed with every curious Tom, Dick and Harry. And he was even more to blame; he should have known better.

Now he had to deal with explaining to his wife just what he'd been doing, lunching there with his former mistress. It didn't take a rocket scientist to imagine what was going through Nena's mind. Of course someone—probably Elisa—would have told her who Luisa was by now. He could hardly blame his cousin's wife. It had been blatantly obvious by the manner in which Luisa communicated with him that there was intimacy between them.

'Damn, damn, damn!' he exclaimed as he rode the elevator up to the suite, glancing at his watch, wishing he could have put off his meeting at the Casa Rosada with the President. But that, of course, would have been impossible. And naturally the President had been late, and the meeting had lasted longer than he'd expected.

And just as everything was going so well, he reflected furiously, when Nena was finally opening up to him like a blooming flower, this had to happen.

He opened the door carefully.

The sitting room of the suite was empty. Then he

moved towards the door of the bedroom and stood in the doorway. But that room was empty too. Hurrying towards the closet, he flung it open, only to have his suspicions confirmed as he confronted a row of empty hangers. She'd gone, he realised, glancing at his watch again and seeing that it was too late to reach the airport in time to impede her flight.

Two minutes later he'd confirmed it with the concierge. So she was off to London. Well, at least that was home territory for her and he knew where to catch up with her. Still, the rift that now loomed between them would be hard to bridge.

Several minutes later he decided the best course of action was to warn his mother and then get himself to London as soon as he could.

Upon arrival at Heathrow Nena went straight to Thurston Manor. The servants were surprised, but glad to see her, and after getting through their greetings and the inevitable congratulations Nena sank onto her old bed, content just to lie there, eyes closed and let go a little of the tension that had travelled with her from Buenos Aires.

She was exhausted, she realised. Not just by the trip, but from the rollercoaster of emotions she'd been through in the past few hours. She hadn't slept during the journey, her mind too taken up with the events of the afternoon to allow her to relax sufficiently to close her eyes. But now, at least, she was home. Really home. Not on *his* territory but on hers, where she called the shots and no one, least of all Ramon, could force her to do anything.

She'd made up her mind what to do on the plane. Tomorrow, once she was more rested, she would phone the lawyers and find out how to go ahead with a divorce. She would not stay married to this man a moment more than necessary. He'd played with her feelings, her heart and her pride and she'd had enough.

For a moment her grandfather flashed before her. But she braced herself. It was too late to worry about her word, which she'd given him. Anyway, she doubted he would have expected Ramon to behave in such a callous, ungentlemanly manner. She could not be expected to just back down, lower her eyes and accept his infidelities like a doormat, could she?

Nena shifted on the bed, too agitated to sleep, too tired to get up and do anything. If only they'd had more time to get to know one another none of this would have happened. Or perhaps she should have paid real attention to that magazine article, shown it to her grandfather. Certainly, she should have asked a few questions before entering naïvely into this wretched arranged marriage.

Finally, after much tossing and turning, Nena managed to fall into a troubled sleep. But her dreams were filled with visions of a tall, dark and handsome man, whose hands created magic when they touched her and for whom, despite all her anger and ire, she still felt desire.

Doña Augusta was a practical woman, and it was frankly no surprise to her when she heard of Nena's sudden return to England. What did surprise her—

actually encouraged her to harbour new hopes for her son—was Ramon's obvious discomfort at the fact. Truth was she had never, in the course of his thirty-two-years, heard him so discomfited.

Well, Augusta thought, as she laid down the telephone receiver, it would do him no harm at all to stew in his own juice for a few days. She was secretly thrilled to know that his relationship with Luisa was terminated. She had never approved of it from the beginning, and had feared that Ramon might, like so many of his peers, get married and continue to live the same life as he had before, paying small heed to his lovely young wife.

But apparently that was not the case.

Gleefully Doña Augusta set about advising her husband of the facts. Not all of them, of course. Just the essentials. There was no earthly use interfering, she pointed out firmly to Don Pedro; it was just important to let Nena know that she had Doña Augusta's friendly ear, should Nena need it. Don Pedro agreed. The couple must, they decided, work it out for themselves.

After having said this, the first thing Doña Augusta did was to invite her daughter-in-law to lunch at Mark's Club *à deux,* where she determined to discover exactly what was going on between the pair. Ramon had been irritatingly vague and Nena excruciatingly polite on the phone. But Doña Augusta sensed that things were in a worse state than she'd let her husband believe. It was time for a little probing, she decided. Not that she meant to interfere, of course, but a little well-placed adjusting could do no harm.

*   *   *

She could hardly refuse the invitation, Nena decided with a sigh. Not that she had the least desire to go to London. As far as she was concerned she could wallow here at Thurston Manor for ever and never show her face again. She felt stupid, ugly and unkempt, and had refused to take any of Ramon's numerous calls. She hadn't washed her hair in days, and her nails needed a serious manicure.

She looked at herself in the mirror, disgusted. Look at what you've become, she threw at herself. With a weary sigh she realised that she couldn't go to lunch looking like this and would simply have to go and have a makeover before meeting her mother-in-law. Reluctantly she picked up the phone and made the necessary appointments.

'So,' Doña Augusta said, settling on the moss green velvet bench of Mark's select dining room, near the window, with Nena seated beside her, 'I hear that you and Ramon have found an apartment in Buenos Aires?'

'Uh, well, we did look at something,' Nena said hesitantly, not wanting to tell Doña Augusta about her decision to get a divorce without first speaking to Ramon. She still hadn't contacted her lawyers, but that, she'd persuaded herself, was because she hadn't had time. After all there had been all those thank-you letters to write for all those wretched wedding presents that she would have gladly packed up and returned.

'Oh, but I thought it was definite?' Augusta raised a perfectly plucked brow.

'Yes—no. Well, it's all rather complicated, to tell you the truth,' Nena conceded. Somehow it was very difficult to look Doña Augusta—the woman who had been so wonderful to her during her grandfather's illness—straight in the eye and tell a blatant lie.

Touching her beautifully coiffed silver hair with a bejewelled hand, Doña Augusta patted Nena's with the other. 'I have the feeling,' she said, taking a sip of crisp champagne, 'that perhaps all is not perfectly harmonious between you and Ramon.'

'Yes, well, no—I mean, it's not really—'

'Nena, I would like you to consider me as a friend rather than your mother-in-law—such a daunting term, isn't it?' she added with a low conspiratorial laugh. 'After all, you have neither your mother nor your grandmother to guide you, *querida*. Let me add, before we go any further, that I have a very realistic view of my son. I am not one of those doting parents who believe their child can do no wrong,' she added firmly. 'I am very well aware of Ramon's—er—faults.'

Nena took a long gulp of champagne. She'd been turning the problem over and over, back and forth in her own mind now for several days. But to open up to Ramon's mother? Would it be right? Would it be wise? Yet as she looked into the other woman's clear grey eyes she suddenly knew she must confide in someone before she went crazy.

'I don't know how to tell you,' she began, staring down at her napkin. 'I thought everything was all right. I was beginning to believe that perhaps the whole idea of our marriage was not such a bad one, and then—' Just the thought of Ramon in Buenos Aires, looking down into Luisa's face as she'd been walking down those steps, left Nena seething, another rush of hot tears ready to be shed.

As though sensing her torment, Doña Augusta laid a hand gently on hers.

'Nena, dear, why don't you just tell me what happened? Keeping it to yourself is far worse. We are women; we need to talk when things bother us. I assure you that what you confide in me will go no further.'

'Well—' Nena took a deep breath '—he has a mistress.'

'Ah! Luisa, I suppose.' Doña Augusta gave a knowing nod. 'Most unsuitable and a thorough nuisance. I had the impression she was on her way out.'

'Not from where I was sitting,' Nena said with a sniff.

'Sitting? You mean you've seen her?'

'Oh, yes,' Nena answered bitterly. 'Rather, I saw *them.*'

'I see.' Doña Augusta's expression turned to consternation. 'Where was that, Nena?'

'At Santi's. Ramon was supposed to be in Cordoba,' she blurted out. 'I went to lunch with Elisa, who'd kindly taken me shopping. I like Santi's, so we went there. It was at the end of the meal, as we were having coffee. I looked up and there he was staring down, smiling at this woman. I knew who she was— I saw them together in that magazine you brought over for Grandfather—I just thought…just imagined that now he was married...' Her voice trailed off and she took another long sip of champagne to ease the pain, though talking about it had made her feel slightly better.

'I'm very sorry you were subjected to that,' Doña Augusta replied, her expression concerned. 'I know from experience that these things are sometimes difficult to deal with. Pedro was quite a Don Juan when we were married, and I had a few run-ins myself. I suppose that is why you came back to London in such a hurry?'

'What else could I do,' Nena replied defensively.

'I'm not criticising,' the older woman responded with a gentle smile. 'In fact I think you did exactly the right thing. It will do Ramon no harm to realise how silly he's been.'

'Doña Augusta, I think it is only fair to warn you— though I wanted to tell him first—that I plan to get a divorce.' Nena held her head up and Doña Augusta noted the determined line of her mouth.

'That is quite a radical decision to take,' the older woman replied carefully.

'I see no future for us under the present circumstances.'

'Of course. But tell me, Nena, what exactly are the present circumstances?'

Nena hesitated. What could she say? That she thought she loved a man who obviously saw her just as a convenience? That to know he was leaving her to see another woman would quite simply kill her?

'Nena, I am much older than you, and so perhaps

am able to have a better inkling of what is going on,'
Doña Augusta said in a smooth, soothing voice.
'Please correct me if I'm wrong, *querida*, but would
I be right in assuming that you have feelings for my
son?'

Swallowing once more, Nena nodded. 'Which is
why it would be impossible to bear,' she murmured,
clasping her hands tight. 'Totally impossible. I know
some women do it, but I couldn't stand seeing him
leave every day, never knowing if—if he was going
to see her.'

'And neither should you have to go through any
such thing,' the older woman replied briskly.

'The best thing is to put an immediate end to the
whole thing,' Nena said with a sigh. 'We never
should have been forced into this situation. It's not
natural. I suppose there was a lot of pressure on
Ramon as well.'

'Rubbish. You are both in it now, and I think you
at least owe each other a chance. A divorce at the first
sign of adversity is for the faint-hearted, Nena, and I
have the impression that you are anything but that,'
she finished shrewdly.

'I don't want to run away, if that's what you mean,'
she replied, squaring her shoulders and sitting up
straighter. She hadn't actually thought of the problem
in this light before.

Doña Augusta contemplated telling Nena what her
son had said on the phone, that the affair with Luisa
was most definitely over. But after a short moment's
reflection she decided not to. It was up to them to

work things out. Still, she considered it time for Ramon to put in an appearance and start fighting for what she was certain he truly wanted. She could hardly wait to see his face when Nena told him she wanted a divorce. It would do him a world of good not to have everything going exactly his way.

It would, indeed.

CHAPTER SIX

'DON RAMON is in the library,' Worthing announced two days later as Nena thankfully finished the last wedding thank-you note.

'Show him in, Worthing,' she said, swallowing, aware that the meeting had to take place and that the sooner she told him of her decision the better.

A minute later Ramon marched into the room. In spite of her resolve, Nena felt her heart lurch when his tall, dark, handsome figure, clad in an immaculate grey suit, entered.

She stood by the window and waited while Worthing closed the door.

'Good morning,' she said, as formally as she could, head held high, her body rigid.

Ramon could read all the tension in her body language. Nena was a little trooper, he realised. She had carried the whole restaurant thing off with such grace and dignity, like the true lady she was. Now, as he watched her across the drawing room, he experienced a surge of admiration—and something else so strong it made him stop and hesitate. It took his breath away and for a moment he remained silent, watching her, thinking what an extraordinary woman she was turning out to be, despite her youth. Then he cleared his throat.

Nena looked him over coldly, hiding her racing pulse, eyes ablaze.

'Why did you run away?' he asked, breaking the silence, with a flash of anger at her sudden disappearance without either his knowledge or permission.

'I should have thought that would have been blatantly obvious,' she replied icily.

'I don't see why you should have gone anywhere.'

'Don't you?' she asked sweetly. 'Well, I'm afraid I disagree. There was obviously not room for me *and* your mistress in Buenos Aires. Apparently we frequent the same establishments,' she threw. 'How very unfortunate.'

'That was bad luck.'

'Really? Well, I'm afraid I don't know the rules of this game, Ramon, and I can't say that I want to learn them. Now that you're here we can discuss the terms of the divorce, once I've seen my lawyers.'

'Divorce?' Ramon took a shocked step forward.

'Yes, divorce. You can't truly expect me to stay married to you after what happened. Surely even *you* can't imagine that I would tolerate that kind of behaviour?'

'Nena, we need to talk about this.'

'No, we don't. The least said the better.'

'Don't be ridiculous.'

'I'm not being ridiculous. I'm being realistic—something that I apparently haven't been over the past few weeks,' she added bitterly, turning away and staring out of the window, through the summer rain and across the lawn.

'Nena, *mi amor,* please—give me a chance to explain.'

'Explain what?' she exclaimed, spinning on her heel. 'That you keep a mistress, a woman who you've been having an affair with for the past couple of years?'

'It's all over.'

'Really? Well, you could have fooled me. I may look young and stupid, Ramon, but I have a minimal amount of brain cells. I find it impossible to believe that you would abandon a woman that you've even been photographed with in *Hola!* magazine, and whom you still see fit to lunch with in the most fashionable restaurant in town, despite the very unimportant fact that you're married,' she replied witheringly.

'Nena, this is absurd,' he said, moving forward and grabbing her arms. 'It was not as you imagine. I had to see Luisa—explain to her. I hadn't advised her properly of our marriage. I owed it to her to take a proper farewell.'

'At Santi's.' Her eyes blazed up at him. 'How dare you treat me like a simpleton?' she threw, pulling away from him, tears burning despite her every effort to quell them. 'How dare you, Ramon?' Before she could stop herself Nena brought the force of her hand across his cheek, then backed off, horrified at her own lack of control.

Ramon stood perfectly still, then raised his hand to his cheek. His face broke into a rueful smile. 'I deserved that. But now, please, calmly, let me explain.'

'No.' She burst into tears. 'I don't want to hear another word about it. Go on—go back to her. She obviously satisfies your every need. I was a fool to think that we—that I—that—' She turned again to the window, shoulders shaking, unable to contain the flow of tears rushing down her cheeks.

'Mi niña,' he said, coming up behind her and slipping his arms around her shaking body. 'There is no need for all this agitation. If only you'd listen to me, let me tell you how things really are—'

'I don't want to know,' she said stubbornly, trying to get out of his arms. 'I don't believe a word of what you say. You're just trying to placate me. Well, I'm not going to be fobbed off.'

He spun her around and faced her, his face set in hard, determined lines. 'I am not a liar, Nena. What happened is unfortunate, but I will not have my wife questioning my word.'

'I didn't say that—'

'Yes, you did. You said you didn't believe me, won't even listen to my version of what happened, and you talk about divorce with the greatest of ease. Is that how you regard marriage?'

His eyes burned into hers and his hands gripped her upper arms. 'I repeat—is that how you view marriage? As something to be thrown out of the window as soon as there is a problem?'

'I—' Nena was taken aback by his sudden change in attitude, and the true and real anger she read in his eyes.

'Answer me,' he ordered, his voice cold and quiet, cutting the silence. 'I want to hear it from your lips.'

Nena swallowed. 'N-no. That is not how I think of marriage. It's just that—'

'Just that what? That you saw me with a woman and presumed I was still sleeping with her?'

Nena felt heat rush to her cheeks.

'Yes.'

'I see. And is there anything else you'd like to share?'

Nena hesitated. 'I don't trust you.'

Ramon drew back, and his face took on a rigid, hard expression. 'I see. Then there is effectively very little for us to talk about. I'll bid you good day.' With a small bow he turned on his heel and marched from the room, leaving Nena standing alone, the wind completely blown out of her sails.

She hadn't meant that—well, not exactly. Perhaps she'd worded it badly. Oh, what had she done? she wondered, remembering the forbidding expression on his face as he'd taken his leave. She hadn't meant to hurt or insult him. And now it was too late. She'd thrown the dice and played her hand and now there was no going back.

A sob caught in her throat and she threw herself on the sofa, where she indulged in a long, stormy cry that brought little relief.

'I want a full report on the Carvajal oil companies,' Ramon told Morton, the late Rodrigo Carvajal's personal secretary, who was now serving as his assistant at the offices of Carvajal Enterprises in Dover Street. 'And get me an audit on the import-export firm too, please.'

'Yes, sir. Will that be all?'

'For the moment, yes. Thanks, Morton.' Ramon looked up and smiled. 'Is Sir Wilfred in yet?'

'He should be in by ten, sir. Shall I tell him you've been asking for him?'

'Please. And Andrew Trenton as well. Do they always come in so late?'

'They usually appear by ten,' Morton replied uncomfortably, sensing disapproval in the new boss's tone.

'Ah, well. That's fine. Please advise them that I need a word, will you?'

'Of course, sir.'

With that Morton withdrew, and Ramon set about going through several thick files. He needed to become totally familiar with all the Carvajal companies and their assets, their management and how they were run. Also, it helped take his mind off Nena.

After their disastrous talk the other day he'd driven back to London and discovered his mother alone in the drawing room in Eaton Square.

'Well, darling? Have you seen Nena?' his mother had asked casually, laying down a copy of *Country Life*.

'I have.'

'And?'

'Not good, I'm afraid. She's talking divorce.' He sat down on the opposite sofa and swung an ankle over his knee. 'I don't know what's the matter with her. It wasn't that terrible after all.'

'Oh? You think that a newly wed bride being faced with her husband's mistress in a restaurant is an everyday occurrence of which she should take no heed?'

'That wasn't what I said,' Ramon replied, irritated. He knew perfectly well he appeared to be in the wrong, and didn't need salt rubbed in the wound.

'Mmm. Then what exactly did you say?'

'That there was no need to make such a to-do about it. She wouldn't even let me explain properly.'

Doña Augusta sent him a long, speculative look. 'Has it occurred to you how that young girl must have felt?'

'Of course it has.'

'Here she is, thrust into a marriage of convenience, having lost her grandfather, whom she adored, dropped into a new society of people she has never seen before, who are considerably older and more sophisticated than she, and from a different culture. And on top of that she's expected to handle a situation like this? Don't you think you're expecting rather a lot?'

'Actually, she handled it brilliantly,' he said, staring at the oriental carpet gracing the hardwood floor. 'She was so dignified and cool you'd have thought she dealt with things like this every day of the week.'

'Good for her. That doesn't mean she's prepared to put up with your lifestyle.'

'I never intended to keep Luisa in my life.'

'You've told me that already,' Doña Augusta said sharply. 'The point is that you don't seem to have made that clear to Nena.'

'She won't listen.'

'If I were you,' Doña Augusta said, rising and picking up her magazine, 'I'd give it a little time and let the dust settle. Life has a funny way of taking care of things.'

Ramon watched her leave the room. He was damned if he'd wait. Yet…his mother had an uncanny way of being right. Oh, well. He would stay here in London and get on with familiarising himself with Don Rodrigo's affairs. After all, he had a moral obligation where they were concerned. He'd given Don Rodrigo his word as a gentleman, and whatever the outcome of his marriage he would not renege on that.

Several days went by, but still Nena hadn't picked up the phone to call her lawyers. She knew that was what she should do, and chided herself for not getting on with it. But somehow every time she was about to look up the number something inexplicable stopped her and she would start thinking about Ramon, about those wonderful, unforgettable nights spent in his arms.

It was absurd and ridiculous to think of them when she knew—perfectly well—that it could never be. She wouldn't be able to live with him knowing he was doing the same things in another bed with another woman. She shuddered, the same mix of pain and anger assailing her. Why, oh, why had she let her heart get involved?

Nena sat at her desk and determinedly filled out applications for several universities. She must think of getting on with her life, of getting an education, instead of mooning over a man who had proved himself worthless and a cheat. But the prospect of college, which before had seemed so thrilling and which she'd longed for so dearly, no longer held the same allure. Plus the past few days she'd been feeling dreadfully tired and listless. Perhaps she should take some vitamins, or something, to boost her metabolism…

But next morning when she woke she felt no better. In fact quite the opposite. Just as she was getting out of bed she found herself rushing to the bathroom, feeling awful. Leaning over the sink, she retched.

The bout of nausea passed and Nena leaned back, staring at her pale face in the mirror. She looked like hell. Oh, well, what did it matter? She'd probably caught some bug in Argentina that had incubated for a while and had now decided to invade her system. As though the place hadn't bugged her enough already. She was very glad to have wiped the dust of it from her shoes. Still, the image of the luscious, sophisticated Luisa gazing up possessively at Ramon kept flashing at odd moments. No wonder she felt sick, she reflected crossly, weaving her way back across the room and collapsing thankfully onto the bed.

At that moment the telephone rang. She very nearly let it be answered downstairs, but then thought better of it.

'Hello?'

'Hello.'

At the sound of Ramon's deep, rich voice, Nena's pulse leaped. How she wished she could get her feelings under control.

'What do you want?' she said, somewhat rudely.

'I was just calling to see if by any chance we could

get together for lunch—say tomorrow? I have a number of things I need to discuss with you.'

He sounded impersonal, almost cold, and Nena felt suddenly downcast. Deep down, he was probably glad to be rid of her.

'What sort of things?' she asked warily.

'Oh, paperwork, a couple of matters concerning the Carvajal oil companies that I think you should be aware of. Particularly if you're going to take over running the companies yourself,' he added coldly.

'I—' It had never occurred to her that if she and Ramon divorced he would hand over his duties. The thought was daunting. 'Well, I suppose we could meet. Where do you want to go?'

'Would Harry's Bar suit you?'

'Fine. What time?' He sounded so dreadfully formal, so distant, as though all they'd shared was somehow in the past.

'A quarter to one?'

'Fine,' she repeated, seeking any kind of change in the tone of his voice.

'I'll see you then.'

He rang off and Nena flopped back against the pillows, wondering why she felt so teary. It was she, after all, who'd suggested the divorce, wasn't it? So what was she whining about? She'd made her bed and now she'd have to lie on it.

Letting out a long sigh, and fighting another bout of nausea, Nena turned on the pillow and buried her head in it. Right now all she wished was for the earth to swallow her up. She'd had enough of facing one wretched thing after another.

But her will got the better of her and soon she was in the shower, determined to remain calm and face whatever was coming with dignity and courage.

Harry's Bar was busy. The waitresses in their pretty uniforms hurried hither and thither, and the sound of social chit-chat reigned as Nena made her way towards a corner table where Ramon was rising to meet her.

She wished he wasn't so handsome, so utterly sexy in his light suit. It was not surprising that most of the women in the place were taking a peek at him out of the corners of their eyes. Some were even quite blatant about it.

'Hello, Nena.' Ramon looked her over, immediately noting how pale and thin she looked.

'Hello, Ramon.'

They didn't kiss, just sort of nodded formally.

'How have you been?' he asked, as though talking politely to a distant acquaintance.

'I'm doing well, thank you. And you?'

'Oh, fine,' he responded.

'And your parents?'

'Fine as well. In fact my mother was wondering whether she could persuade you to come for dinner tonight at Eaton Square.'

'Oh, I don't think I—' Nena said hurriedly, then, remembering how kind Doña Augusta had been, felt bad.

'It would give them great pleasure,' Ramon said, pushing every button he knew might pressure her into staying. 'I can always pick you up, if it's too long for you to remain in town all that time.'

'All right, I'll come.'

'Then we could meet somewhere and I'll drive you over there.'

'That's perfectly all right, thank you,' she said, dismissing his offer. 'I have a number of things to get done this afternoon. You can pick me up at Chester Square.'

'Fine. At seven.'

The next few minutes were spent studying the menu. Nena wondered what she should eat. The nausea had passed, but she feared that should she make the wrong choice it might return, and the last thing she wanted was to make a scene. In the end she declined a starter and opted for some grilled chicken and vegetables.

Ramon quirked a brow. 'No shrimp cocktail? I seem to recall you liked that.'

'No—no, thanks,' Nena replied hurriedly, the mere thought of the stuff making her queasy. 'I'm not very hungry today.'

'I see. Well, you must take care of your health. You look a little off-colour.'

'Oh, it's nothing. Just a bug I think I must have picked up somewhere. It'll pass.'

He sent her a long, piercing look but made no comment.

'What are the things you need to talk to me about?' she asked, tentatively sipping her champagne, hoping it wouldn't have dire effects upon her queasy system.

He frowned. 'Talk about? Oh, yes. Well, there are

a couple of matters that you should be aware of. In fact, if you are considering taking a participating interest in the Carvajal companies I think you should spend some time in the office becoming familiar with them. I was going to bring a couple of files with me, but then I thought better of it. Easier for you to come to Dover Street and look them over at a desk.'

'I see.' And she did, in more ways than one.

A tiny flutter circled her heart and she peered at him from under her thick lashes. He looked so cold, so formal, his mouth set in a determined line and that arrogant head held high. But she couldn't help wondering if perhaps, despite the forbidding countenance, he hadn't arranged this lunch as an excuse to see her. The thought sent a thrill coursing through her and she took another quick sip of champagne, surprised to see that her glass was almost empty.

Before she could protest Ramon had ordered another one. Oh, well. She might need it at this rate.

She was lovely. Though so pale and waif-like. Nena was a proud woman and he'd hurt her—not only her feelings, but her self esteem, Ramon realised. He of all people knew how much that could rankle. The good news was that she apparently hadn't gone ahead with any phone calls to lawyers regarding the divorce she'd talked of. Perhaps she was thinking better of it. Living without her, spending his days cloistered in the office and nights alone in his bed in Eaton Square, recalling how they'd made love together, were not proving easy to handle.

He eyed her cool, calm and collected front. She

was quite an adversary, he realised ruefully, but one he was determined to vanquish in the end.

But these thoughts he kept to himself.

By the end of lunch Nena was amazed that they'd ended up chit-chatting about this and that in a surprisingly relaxed manner. She pulled herself up with a bang. This man was dangerous, far too smooth an operator. She must be careful and try and know her own mind, she reflected crossly as she walked into the Harvey Nichols department store later that afternoon. After all, hadn't she decided what she wanted?

With a sigh—because she obviously hadn't—Nena headed to the designer floor, and without much interest began looking at clothes.

Dining at Eaton Square was a potentially embarrassing situation, Nena realised uneasily as she lingered in the bath. What did Don Pedro and Doña Augusta think about all that was happening? After all, it was obvious all was not right between her and Ramon, since they were living apart. Her mother-in-law had seemed very tolerant of the whole thing. But what about Don Pedro? Would he express recrimination at her abandoning the conjugal domicile?

But Nena's fears were immediately allayed by the warm reception she received. Ramon had phoned and suggested he pick her up on foot, as it was just around the corner and the evening was lovely. And she'd agreed. She could think of nothing nicer than a walk before dinner.

Soon they'd arrived at the mansion on the corner of Eaton Square. Once again Nena was impressed by the exquisitely decorated rooms, the collection of paintings hung on the stairs and the more contemporary works in the vast living room.

'How lovely to see you, Nena.' Don Pedro welcomed her with a broad smile and drew her next to him on the sofa. 'We have missed you the past few days. But I'm certain you must be very busy, with much to do at Thurston.'

'Uh, yes,' she said, grateful to him for making it look as if the separation were a natural one, forced by circumstance rather than the rift that existed between Ramon and herself. Eyeing her mother-in-law out of the corner of her eye, she wondered just how much she'd told her husband. And appreciated Doña Augusta's obvious discretion, glad that she was proving to be the friend she'd professed.

Nena felt a rush of affection. There had been no older woman in her life since the untimely death of her grandmother four years earlier—no one to talk to or to seek advice from. Suddenly, knowing that Doña Augusta had really meant what she'd said the other day at lunch made her feel better. Perhaps she could talk to the older woman about how rotten she was feeling physically. Of course she could always go to Dr Grainger, the family physician in Harley Street, but for some reason she didn't want to. Perhaps the best thing, she decided as she chatted with Don Pedro, laughing at his jokes and feeling more at ease, was to let it cure itself.

Ramon was at his most charming. She could feel his eyes on her practically all the time, and she blushed. It was impossible not to remember, not to long for what he'd taught her, what he'd wakened within her.

By the end of an excellent dinner in such pleasant surroundings Nena felt positively sad that it was time to leave. She was very fond of Ramon's parents, and appreciated the kind way they'd embraced her into their family. She wished—oh, how she wished—that things might have been different.

But they weren't, she reminded herself as Ramon prepared to escort her back to Chester Square.

Night was just beginning to fall as they stepped outside, even though it was nearly ten o'clock. They began walking and Ramon slipped his arm in hers. Nena stiffened, then realised it would be churlish to reject what was probably nothing more than a gentle-manly gesture, and together they proceeded. Soon they were passing St Michael's Church, and nearing her front door. Ramon slowed.

'Nena, would you mind if I came inside and we had a talk?' he asked, his expression softer than it had been all day. 'I know you're very angry with me, and I deserve that, but I think you owe me the courtesy of listening to my side of the story.'

'Does it have to be tonight?' she enquired, looking away, wondering how she could avoid the inevitable confrontation. It was bad enough having him so close, breathing the scent of him—musky cologne mixed with that unforgettable male scent she'd remember for as long as she lived.

'Well?' Ramon quirked his dark brow at her, eyes piercing hers, filled with determination.

He was not going to be fobbed off, Nena realised,

giving in despite her reluctance. 'Okay,' she said with a shrug. 'You might as well come in and have a nightcap.'

'Don't sound so enthusiastic about it,' he murmured, making her smile in spite of everything.

'Sorry—I didn't mean to sound unwelcoming. I'm just rather tired tonight.'

'You look tired,' he said as they walked up the front steps and she pulled out her key, not waiting for the servants to come to the door. 'Are you sure you're okay?'

'Fine. Just that bug, I think. I'll be better in a couple of days. Nothing to worry about,' she replied as he held the door for her to pass into the hall.

'I certainly hope so. I don't want you getting ill.'

'It's really none of your business any longer,' she said, raising her determined chin and facing him.

Ramon stiffened and his eyes blazed. 'You are still my wife,' he uttered bitingly, 'and as such you are under my protection.'

'Oh, don't be so archaic,' Nena countered, surprised at his reaction.

'Archaic?' Ramon took a step forward. 'That may very well be. But I'll remind you that I'm your husband and it is therefore my right to be informed about your wellbeing.'

He was standing over her now, looking down into her face, eyes hard and gleaming, his mouth set in a harsh, determined line that left no room for argument. And Nena was unable to take her eyes away from his, unable to pull away, to flee the hypnotic gaze riveting her to the spot.

Before she could react his hand touched her cheek. It trailed to her lips. Then just as suddenly she was in his arms and his mouth came down on hers, crushing, forcing open her lips, demanding her to bend to his will.

For a moment Nena resisted—pushed her fists against his chest and tried to escape his hold. Then all at once his tongue touched a spot so sensitive, so tender and so vulnerable that all she could do was allow him to press her against him, feel the hardness of his body and his desire, and submit, allow his hands to roam down her back, knead her neck, and possessively caress the curve of her buttocks.

'I want you,' he growled when he came up for breath. 'God, how I want you, my Nena, how I've missed you. Come upstairs and let's finish what we've begun.'

'I—I thought you wanted to talk,' she gasped, trying to compose herself long enough to regain her sanity.

'We can do that afterwards—whenever,' he responded, pushing her firmly towards the stairs.

'No. No. Ramon, wait.' She pushed her hands against his chest and took a step back. 'This is all so simple for you, isn't it? Just kiss and make up and we'll all be friends and a happy little family again. Well, it isn't that simple. Not for me, at any rate,' she said hoarsely, her heart beating so hard she could almost hear it. 'I am not about to become some kind of carpet for you to walk all over. If you wanted us to be an item you should have thought your life out before we got married, not afterwards.'

'You're being childish and petty,' he replied, unwilling to give up.

'Maybe. But for now that's how I feel.'

'What about the divorce? I haven't had any calls from your lawyers as yet,' he challenged, eyes gleaming with contempt. 'Empty threats, Nena, not so easy to follow up on when it comes to the crunch, are they?'

'Is that what you think?' She drew back and glared at him, feeling foolish and belittled. 'Then, very well, you shall hear from my lawyers, if that is what you want.'

'I never said that, so stop trying to put words into my mouth.'

'Yes, you did. You said—'

Ramon stepped forward and in one swift movement pulled her hard against him. 'I married you for better or worse, not for you to walk out as soon as the going got rough,' he spat angrily. Then before Nena could move he'd crushed her mouth under his again and forced her to open to him.

It was so hard to resist, so awfully hard, and Nena found herself yielding when every instinct told her not to. Then his hand found her breast and fondled it. Not gently, but expertly, leaving her wet and wanting, her legs buckling as his hand came swiftly down and he touched that most sensitive spot of her body, which reacted even through the fabric of her dress and panties. Then, as she gasped, he drew away.

'A very good night to you, *señora mia.* I hope you enjoy your lonely bed.'

With that he turned on his heel and, letting himself

out, marched down the front steps and walked furiously in the direction of Eaton Square.

Nena sank onto the third step of the long flight of stairs and let out a tiny moan. It was all so confusing, so difficult to contend with. One minute she wanted to loathe him, the next to love him. The feel of his hands on her body had awakened every nerve, set alight every sensation. Now she stared at the closed door, asking herself what on earth was going to happen next. He'd almost dared her to call her lawyer—yet he'd touched her and kissed her in such a way that—

It was all too frustrating! And he was impossible. Entirely impossible.

Steadying herself on the banister, Nena rose, and trailed upstairs. In her room she undressed slowly, eyeing her body in the mirror as she undressed, touching the spot on her breast where his fingers had left a mark, seeing her nipples aroused, swollen with naked desire. She could feel the soft dampness between her thighs and closed her eyes, wishing, longing for one lingering, dreamy moment that she'd given in, let him stay, let him come upstairs and make love to her, let him ease this delicious ache that persisted, begging for completion.

Then common sense asserted itself and she turned her eyes away and grabbed an old pair of flannel pyjamas. At least they weren't sexy, didn't remind her of the honeymoon, of the way he'd told her to remove her nightdress and how deliciously sensual, how powerful she'd suddenly felt, standing naked before him.

Stop it, she ordered, marching into the bathroom

and squirting toothpaste onto her brush. She was acting like a brainless idiot, like those girls she'd so despised at school who had always been drooling over men. Surely she had more self-control than that?

But as she slipped between the covers, with the scent and feel of Ramon still impinged upon her brain and her being, Nena wondered if she had any sense left at all.

The best thing was to try and get a decent night's sleep, she decided, switching off the light and staring out of the window. Perhaps he was sleepless too, and not five minutes away, she reflected, tossing in the bed, eyeing the starry night.

It was all so desperately frustrating, she concluded, letting go an irritated sigh. And the worst part was she'd asked for it by not even allowing him to tell her what his version of the Luisa tale was.

Suddenly Nena sat up in bed, her hair falling wildly about her shoulders. What if it was actually true and he *had* been seeing Luisa for the last time?

'Oh, hell!' she exclaimed, punching her pillow angrily. She was sick and tired of this game, and the sooner it was over the better off they'd all be.

'Well?'

Ramon saw his mother mounting the wide flight of stairs as he entered the hall and hesitated.

'Well, nothing. I dropped Nena off, that's all,' he replied curtly.

'I gathered that,' Doña Augusta said patiently. 'How are things between the two of you?'

'If you want the truth, I have no damn idea,'

Ramon exploded. 'And please don't go on about it, Mother. I've had just about enough of this whole nonsense. Did you see how Nena looked? How unwell? It's ridiculous, the way she's behaving.'

'She did strike me as somewhat pale,' Doña Augusta agreed, coming back down the stairs and leading the way to the sitting room. 'Perhaps I'd better ring her tomorrow and see if she's all right.'

'Well, I hope you get a better reception than I did,' he muttered, heading straight for the silver drinks tray and pouring himself a stiff brandy. 'There's just so much of Nena's nonsense I'm prepared to tolerate,' he added through gritted teeth. 'I've had about enough of her antics.'

'Maybe she's had enough of yours,' Doña Augusta murmured, disguising a smile at her son's fury.

'Whatever. Either way, this ridiculous situation has to be put a stop to one way or another. I'm damned if I'm having my wife sleep under her own roof. It's disgraceful.'

'Tell me, *querido*, just out of interest, is it your heart or your pride that is suffering most right now?' his mother asked casually. 'That is perhaps a matter you should ask yourself.'

'Oh, Mother, leave me alone, please. I'm not in the mood for philosophical conversations. I'm off to bed.'

'Goodnight, my son. Sweet dreams.'

'Goodnight,' Ramon muttered, then stalked from the room, leaving Doña Augusta staring into the empty fireplace, a smile twitching the corner of her lips.

CHAPTER SEVEN

'DOÑA AUGUSTA is in the living room,' the maid said as Nena made her way downstairs. She felt washed out, and the bouts of sickness hadn't stopped as she'd believed they would. Could she have something serious? she wondered, taking a deep breath as she reached the hall. What was Doña Augusta doing here at ten-thirty in the morning? She felt rather dizzy, and disinclined to talk, but could hardly turn her mother-in-law out.

'Nena.' Doña Augusta rose from the sofa and Nena went over to kiss her. 'Sit down, child, and tell me what is wrong with you,' she said immediately. 'You look very pale and unwell. Have you seen a doctor?'

'No. I haven't. I don't know what's wrong with me. For several days now I've felt so queasy, but only when I wake up. By the end of the morning I feel so much better that I think I'm on the mend. I think I must have caught some sort of bug,' she said gloomily.

'Only in the morning, you say?' Doña Augusta asked casually.

'Yes. It's the oddest thing. I can't bear the thought of breakfast, but by lunchtime I'm quite hungry.'

'Hmm. Excuse me asking you something so personal, *querida,* but when did you last have your period?'

'Oh, I don't know—a few weeks ago.' Nena closed her eyes a moment and waited for the wave of dizziness to pass. 'I'm sorry,' she said. 'I'll be fine in a minute.'

Doña Augusta smiled. The child had no idea what was happening to her, she realised ruefully, wondering how the news would affect the situation between Ramon and her, and knowing she must tread carefully.

'Nena, have you thought that perhaps it might not be a bug?'

'Well, no. I don't really see what else it could be.' Then all at once Doña Augusta's previous question rang loud and clear in her head and she sat up straighter. 'Oh! You don't think that I might be—?' She turned towards her mother-in-law, her eyes wide.

'Expecting a baby?' she asked softly.

'But I can't be. I mean, these things don't happen just like that, do they?'

'That depends. Have you been using any form of contraception?'

'Uh, no. I didn't think about it. I—'

'Well, in that case I think there is a strong possibility that you may be pregnant. Morning sickness is one of the first symptoms. I had it dreadfully when I was expecting Ramon.'

Nena sat on the sofa in shock. Pregnant. Expecting Ramon's baby. What was she going to do?

'Doña Augusta, please don't tell Ramon. At least until I've found out for sure if I am really pregnant.

Things aren't—well, you know they're not—going too well between us now. I need to be able to make my own decisions.'

'I understand, my dear, but let me make an appointment for you with an excellent gynaecologist. He will be able to tell you if you are expecting or not, and then we'll take it from there. As for now, I want you to lie down on the sofa and put your legs up. Here.' Doña Augusta placed another cushion behind Nena's back. 'And some herb tea might help. I'll get the maid to make some immediately,' she said, taking charge.

A baby.

What would it be like? Was it a boy or a girl? And what if she and Ramon—? The thought didn't bear thinking about. How would he react if she was pregnant? This couldn't have come at a worse time, she decided, caught between the newborn emotions of imagining a tiny person growing inside her womb and the fact that she and Ramon were so torn apart.

She sighed, closed her eyes and let Doña Augusta fuss, ordering tea and covering her legs with a cashmere throw before she headed for the telephone and began making calls.

Several minutes later she returned to Nena's side. 'Good. I have got you an appointment for tomorrow morning at eleven. I can come with you, but quite understand if you would prefer to go alone.'

'Thank you.' Nena smiled gratefully. 'If you don't mind, I think I'd better go by myself.'

'I understand, *querida*. But please phone me when he tells you the result.'

'And you won't tell Ramon?'

'Didn't I promise this would remain our secret? That is on the condition that you allow me to take proper care of you. After all, you may be expecting my grandchild,' she added with a conspiratorial smile.

'Of course. You've been wonderful. Thank you so much.'

'Not at all. I'm thrilled to finally have a daughter to spoil.'

'Yes,' Nena replied hesitantly. What if she and Ramon split up? What then?

But right now she mustn't think of that, must just get through the rest of the day, then go to the doctor and find out the truth. There would be time then to find answers to the rest of her dilemmas.

There was something wrong with the numbers.

Ramon frowned. He'd been over the audits several times and something didn't fly. He picked up the pages where he'd circled several items in red and re-viewed them once more. And that wasn't all, he re-flected, leaning back in the leather swivel chair. He had a feeling there were other issues going on at management level in several of Don Rodrigo Carvajal's companies. But as yet he hadn't pinned them down, and he was loath to show his hand before he was certain of his facts.

And it might take him a little time to find out.

He didn't trust the urbane Sir Wilfred, with his suave, ready answers and slightly patronising attitude. In fact he wondered for just how long he'd been rip-ping Don Rodrigo off. Too long, probably. Certainly since the old gentleman had become ill and had been obliged to hand over the everyday running of his affairs to the man. Then there was that team of high-powered savvy lawyers, who seemed to have an excessive amount of power within the structure of the holding company.

It would take him some sleuthing, but Ramon was determined to get to the bottom of it. Still, these problems, and a number of others he was dealing with in his own affairs back home, did not stop him from wondering just how he was going to handle the biggest problem of all: his wife.

Nena was being recalcitrant and difficult. He'd thought yesterday that she would finally listen to him, allow him to explain, and that maybe they could get over the hurdle that had risen between them. He thought of her, pliant and yielding in his arms, and his body reacted immediately. She was lovely. That she should believe he could possibly want another woman when he had her was almost amusing. But that was precisely what Nena thought, that he had married her out of convenience—which he had—and that he planned to continue with his old life as well.

The other thing worrying him was the state of her health. She'd seemed better last night, but when he'd phoned half an hour ago to talk to her, in the hope that he might persuade her to meet him for lunch, the maid had said she was unwell and couldn't be disturbed.

Suddenly Ramon got up. This was ridiculous. If she was ill then he must get her to the doctor. Grabbing his suit jacket from the back of the chair, he slipped it on and made his way out of the office.

'I'll be back later, Miss Brown. Please advise Morton,' he told Don Rodrigo's dragon-like secretary, who sat behind a large desk, ramrod-straight, wearing a pair of horn-rimmed glasses that made her look like an owl.

'Very well, sir.'

'I'll phone in and you can tell me if there are any important calls. Is Sir Wilfred in yet?'

'No, sir. He has a meeting in the City this morning, with the American bankers for Carvajal Oil.'

'But I specifically said I needed to be at that meeting.' Ramon frowned, torn between his desire to go to Nena and the knowledge that he should definitely stay and be informed of what was going on. 'Damn it. Why wasn't I advised?'

'I'm afraid I only learned the news by chance myself, sir.' Miss Brown pursed her lips, and for the first time she exchanged a long glance with him.

'I see. Well, in future I think we should keep our eyes and ears well open, Miss Brown,' Ramon responded carefully, mindful of the fact that Miss Brown, like Morton, had worked for over thirty years with Don Rodrigo, who had held the highest opinion of her. If he had to trust someone, she was certainly his best bet.

Turning on his heel, he took the ancient cage elevator down to the ground floor, then grabbed a taxi. Nena would just have to wait. The issues at hand were too important to let slip. It would do no harm for the

Americans to know he was actively on board at Carvajal, and that from now on they'd be dealing with him.

In the doctor's office Nena slipped her clothes back on, returned from behind the screen and sat down on the opposite side of Dr Langtry's desk.

'Just a few minutes, Mrs Carvajal, while we verify the test. All your symptoms seem to indicate that you are expecting a baby, but we'd better be certain.' He smiled at her and she smiled back weakly, her mind in a frenzy as little by little the reality of the whole thing sank in.

At that moment the nurse entered and handed him a slip of paper.

'Thank you.' The doctor skimmed over the results.

'Well, Mrs Carvajal, see for yourself,' he said handing her the typed piece of paper. 'You are expecting a baby for next April.'

Hand trembling, Nena stared at the word 'positive'. She swallowed. Was she happy? Sad? Or just overwhelmed?

'Thank you, Doctor,' she said hoarsely.

'Come back in two weeks and we'll see how you're faring. The morning sickness should pass after the first three months, maybe sooner. Dry toast and tea is the best remedy. But then you must eat properly—plenty of vegetables and nourishing food—and lots of exercise, of course. I recommend swimming and walking.'

'What about tennis?' Nena asked weakly.

'You mentioned slight pain, so I'd say nothing too vigorous just at the moment.'

'Okay.' Nena nodded.

Five minutes later she was seated in the back of her grandfather's Bentley, wondering what to do. She must tell Doña Augusta, but what about Ramon? Would he assume that this simply obliterated the problems they had? Would he see this as a way of sorting things out exactly as he wanted?

Nena experienced a sudden pang of hunger and knew she simply must eat roast beef. Odd. She'd never been very partial to roast beef, but now the mere thought of it made her mouth water and she could barely think of anything else.

All at once her mobile phone rang.

'Hello?'

'Hi, it's me. I've been looking for you.'

'Who's me?' she asked haughtily, her lips twitching. He was so dreadfully arrogant and presumptuous she couldn't resist.

'What are you doing for lunch?'

'Eating roast beef.' The words were out before she could stop herself.

'Eating roast—? Well, all right. Why don't I join you? Where are you?'

'I'm in the car, coming up to Piccadilly Circus.'

'Then meet me at Wilton's. I'll be there in twenty minutes.'

'But—' Nena was about to say that she didn't know if she wanted to lunch with him, then gave up. Frankly, the roast beef was more important, and Wilton's certainly prepared some of the best in town.

The car drew up in Jermyn Street and she alighted and entered the restaurant.

'I believe my—my husband—' the word still caught on her lips '—phoned to reserve a table,' she said to the *maître d'*.

'Why, of course, Mrs Villalba. This way, please.'

Nena followed him through the restaurant and was shown into one of the booths, where she sat down thankfully. She was about to order a glass of champagne, then hesitated. Alcohol wasn't good for the baby.

'Some mineral water, please. Still.'

All at once it wasn't just her desires and wishes that counted any longer. She had a being inside her whom she must protect and shield from harm. The thought sent a wave of emotion coursing through her. Instinctively she touched her belly and took a deep breath. But she still had no inkling of what she would tell Ramon.

Then he was standing there, leaning over her, and her heart did a somersault. As he sat down on the opposite banquette she looked over at him, this man whom despite everything she longed for—and the father of her child, she reminded herself unsteadily.

'Ah. Champagne, Nena?'

'No, thanks. I'll just stick to water for now.'

Ramon frowned. 'Are you still feeling unwell?' he asked, eyes filled with concern.

'No, no. I'm fine, actually. Just rather hungry.'

'I see. Well, that's a good sign. I suppose we'd better order right away. Is the roast beef still on?'

'Absolutely.' She laughed, and they smiled at each other, their eyes lingering. 'With all the trimmings.'

Ramon ordered, then watched her. She looked

tense and he wondered what was troubling her. Surely not just the problems they were facing? She hadn't mentioned the divorce again, and had seemed quite amenable to having lunch. But he would not repeat pushing matters too fast too soon. It might pay off to retreat a little.

'I'll be going away for a few days,' he remarked casually, after the waiter had served him a glass of wine.

'Oh? Where are you going. Back to Buenos Aires?' He caught the edge in her voice and smothered a smile.

'No. Actually, I'm going to New York. I need to visit your grandfather's office there, and deal with some personal business of my own as well.'

'I see.' Nena waited a moment, then experienced a sudden flash of disappointment that he hadn't asked her to join him. Not that she would have gone, of course, but he could have at least asked.

'No wine?' Ramon asked.

'No, thanks.' Nena glanced at the bottle and felt her tummy flip at the mere thought of the stuff.

'Are you sure you're all right?' Ramon queried, his brows creasing once more. She'd looked rather green at the mention of the wine and he wondered why.

Nena's brain was working nineteen to the dozen now.

'When are you leaving?' she asked, torn between telling him her news now or waiting till he got back and she'd made up her mind what she wanted to do.

'I'm flying out tomorrow morning.'

'I see. And how long do you plan to stay in New York?'

'A few days. Not sure exactly how many,' he added casually. 'It depends on what's going on over there. I might take the weekend and pop over to Newport. I have friends who own a beautiful sloop. She's sailed in the Americas Cup. I thought I might fit in a little sailing.'

Nena leaned back, trying to control her emotions. Here she was, with the biggest piece of news to hit her young life, and he was going sailing. She might have known it. Well, let him go sailing, and whatever else he planned to do. What did she care? She was damned if she was going to tell him now. Let him wait.

The roast beef arrived, but for some inexplicable reason she seemed to have lost her appetite.

'I thought you were desperately hungry, *querida?* What happened?' Ramon asked innocently, noting the slight glare in her eyes.

'I'm fine. I must have just misjudged my own appetite.' She sent a bright, brittle smile across the table and began to talk of inconsequential mundane subjects.

'Are you sure you'll be all right while I'm away?' he asked, as they finally rose from the table.

'Of course,' she scoffed. 'Why shouldn't I be?'

'I don't know.' He shrugged and sent her a rueful smile. 'No reason.'

Outside the restaurant Nena's car was waiting. 'Do you want a lift to Dover Street?'

'No, thanks, I'll walk.'

'Fine. Then *bon voyage*.'

'Thanks. I'll see you when I get back.' He dropped a light kiss on her cheek and saw her into the vehicle.

'He'll see me when he gets back,' Nena muttered angrily to herself, watching his tall, broad-shouldered figure march off down the street. 'We'll see about that.'

But she had to admit that it was awfully comforting to know he was at the helm of all her grandfather's affairs, that she was not left high and dry in the hands of those suave, well-spoken lawyers whom she didn't understand half the time and whom for some reason she didn't entirely trust.

Then she remembered Doña Augusta, and sighed. She felt bad about telling anyone of her pregnancy before she told Ramon. But then she'd had her chance and hadn't taken it. Oh, well. She supposed there was nothing for it but to confide in the older woman and hope she wouldn't tell him. Somehow she felt that she could trust her mother-in-law. There was something very trustworthy about Doña Augusta. And she had the feeling that what she'd said was true—she had a surprisingly unbiased and realistic opinion of her own son.

Slowly she picked up the mobile and arranged to pop over to Eaton Square, where a few minutes later Doña Augusta was waiting for her.

'Come in, my dear. Let's have a cup of tea in the sitting room.' She gave the order to the butler, then accompanied Nena into a small, intimate room, decorated with flowered cushions and a window seat, that was obviously her own private little enclave.

'How pretty this is!' Nena exclaimed.

'Well, I have to have somewhere that is feminine in a house full of male energy,' her mother-in-law replied, laughing. 'Now sit down, *querida*, and tell me what the doctor said.'

Nena sat obediently on one of the plump sofas and took a deep breath.

'It's true,' she said in a rush. 'I'm pregnant. He says the baby will be born in April.'

'Well, many congratulations, my love. That is wonderful news. When do you plan to tell Ramon?'

'I don't know. It's—it's all so difficult. I thought of telling him at lunch, but—'

'You lunched together?'

'Yes. At Wilton's. I felt like roast beef.'

'Ah!'

'Oh, I don't know what to do.' Suddenly Nena burst into a flood of unbidden tears that she couldn't control. 'I d-don't know what's the matter with me,' she hiccuped, feeling for a non-existent hanky. 'I'm never up and down like this—all undecided. It's as if my reasoning mind has flown out the window.'

'But, Nena, *mi querida,* that is only natural.' Doña Augusta sat next to her on the sofa and took her hand. 'When we are expecting a baby all our emotions change. We cry for no reason, see things as black when in fact they're not, and have all sorts of unexpected feelings. Remember, your body and your mind are acclimatising to being a mother. It is no longer you alone, but the two of you to be taken care of.'

Nena sniffed and nodded. 'I know. I thought about that today in the restaurant.'

'So tell me,' Doña Augusta said soothingly, 'why didn't you tell him?'

'Because he said he was going to New York and then going sailing in Newport. Sailing! Can you imagine? I mean, what does he need to go sailing for? Why can't he just come—?' Realising suddenly how foolish she must sound, Nena clamped her mouth shut.

'Perhaps you have not shown him that you want him back,' her mother-in-law murmured softly. 'Men have a funny way of retiring into their shells. They can be very proud. Did you let Ramon talk to you about what happened in BA?'

Nena shook her head and stared at her hands. 'No. I didn't.'

'You won't be cross with me if I say that was perhaps a little foolish? He deserved to be punished, I agree. And I'm sure it did him a world of good to know he couldn't have everything his own way. But I honestly believe he was telling the truth when he said his affair with Luisa was over.'

'Do you?' Nena turned her big streaming eyes, filled with tears and uncertainty, towards her. 'But she's so lovely, so beautiful, so worldly and sophisticated. I can see why he'd want to be with her rather than with me. After all, I'm really just a commitment he took on.' She swallowed. 'I didn't realise that I would—'

'Fall in love?' her mother-in-law supplied gently, a tender smile curving her lips. 'Why not? I fell in love with my husband after we were married. And I have good reason to believe he did the same. Has it never occurred to you, Nena, that Ramon might be in love with you?'

'No. Of course not. I mean, why should he be? If you'd seen the way he and Luisa were looking at each other, like a couple—I'm sure he loves her.'

'Rubbish,' Doña Augusta dismissed briskly. 'Luisa and he were good companions. They frequented the same crowd, and all that, and I'm sure they had a well-attuned sex-life together while it lasted. But that's not what I'm referring to. I'm talking about passion, about true love—that feeling that comes once in a lifetime and never lets go.'

'Well, if he loves me why would he go off to New York and stay for the weekend for his wretched sailing when he doesn't have to?' she muttered, sniffing, and accepting the hanky Doña Augusta handed her.

'Because you've been holding him at arm's length, *querida*. What man wouldn't salvage his pride at some point? Particularly an arrogant, self-confident creature like Ramon. This has probably never happened to him before.'

'I suppose not,' Nena answered dully.

'Now, my recommendation is that you go home, relax, and take this week to think out very clearly what it is you want to do. Then when he gets back you can decide.'

'You're probably right,' Nena murmured dejectedly. 'And you won't tell him about the baby, will you?' she asked, suddenly worried.

'Of course not, *querida*. It will be our secret until the time you decide to reveal it. That is your privilege,' Doña Augusta added, smiling and squeezing

Nena's hand. 'And if you need me—and even if you don't,' she added ruefully, 'I shall be close by, making sure you're all right.'

After tea Nena went home, feeling a little calmer but very tired. She was meant to be having dinner with her old schoolfriends, Venetia and Tania, but she felt suddenly too tired, exhausted by the emotions of the day, and ready to make it an early night.

As the plane took off Ramon nursed a whisky and gazed down through the summer drizzle at the landscape below. There was much to be straightened out, and he had every intention of settling matters as soon as he could. Still, an uneasy feeling accompanied him as he leaned back in the wide, comfortable seat and pondered on all that had occurred over the past few weeks.

Nena had seemed so up and down yesterday—not her usual self at all. But there was little use worrying about it. He'd be much better served by studying the files he'd brought with him.

With a sigh Ramon opened his briefcase and settled in for the long flight. At least it would give him time to review all the issues that were worrying him about Carvajal's, and which he needed to get to the bottom of.

Plus, a week away from Nena might not do either of them any harm. As long as she was more amenable by the time he got back…

CHAPTER EIGHT

THREE nights later Nena woke in the middle of the night conscious of a stabbing pain in her lower abdomen. At first she turned over and tried to find a more comfortable position in the bed and go back to sleep. But when it persisted—got stronger—she became worried.

Switching the bedside lamp on, she tried to sit up, but simply doubled over. Then as she removed the bedcovers and tried to lower her feet to the ground she suddenly realised she was bleeding.

'Oh, no,' she uttered, horrified. What could be happening to her? Surely she couldn't be losing the baby?

Cold fear gripped her as she sat on the edge of the bed, perfectly still, as though by doing so she could somehow stop the upheaval occurring inside her body. Then another twinge had her gasping. Instinctively she reached as best she could for the phone, while falling back against the pillows.

After several deep breaths she rang the Villalba number and waited anxiously for someone to answer the phone.

'Hello?'

Don Pedro's voice reached her down the line and she squirmed, wishing it had been Doña Augusta who'd answered. This was so embarrassing—phoning in the middle of the night. What would her father-in-law think? Though frankly she was past caring.

'It's Nena,' she answered, her voice tremulous. 'I'm so sorry to disturb you so late,' she said breathlessly. 'Is—is Doña Augusta there?'

'Of course she's here—but, Nena,' he said, suddenly coming fully awake, 'is something the matter?'

'Yes—well, could I speak to her?'

'Of course, my dear, at once.' She heard him murmuring something to his wife as he passed the phone.

'Nena, tell me what is wrong?' Doña Augusta asked anxiously.

'I—well, I woke up with this awful pain, and it's not getting better. And then when I sat up I realised I was—well, that I was bleeding,' she said in a rush.

'Oh, my goodness. Stay right where you are and I shall be there in a few minutes. In the meantime don't move. I shall call an ambulance immediately.'

'Ambulance?' Nena said hoarsely.

'Yes. You must be taken to hospital at once, my love, or you may lose the baby.'

'Oh, no.' Nena felt tears surfacing once more. 'Oh, please God, no. I want this baby so much. I—'

'Calm down, Nena, it will be all right. We'll be there as soon as we can.'

Nena hung up and stayed motionless against the pillows, tears coursing down her cheeks. How could she have been so idiotic? Why hadn't she told Ramon about the baby? Now maybe it would be too late. Nena closed her eyes and tried to stay calm. For the baby's sake, she kept repeating to herself. For that tiny, crucial wisp of life growing inside her that she was determined to preserve whatever the cost.

Several minutes later she heard footsteps on the landing and a knock on the door.

'Come in.'

'Ah, Nena.' Doña Augusta came hurrying across the room, having been let in by Worthing, who was now waiting for the ambulance. 'My poor child. Now stay quiet. We will go with you to the hospital.'

'We?' Nena asked in a small voice.

'I had to tell Pedro, I'm afraid.'

'Oh, never mind.' Nena smiled as best she could and closed her eyes as another pain loomed. 'It doesn't matter any longer.'

'There, that's better,' Doña Augusta soothed. 'We'll be at the hospital very shortly, and all will be well, I'm certain. But in the future we must take better care of you.'

Ramon felt his cellphone vibrating and excused himself to Grant Connelly, the high-flying New York attorney he was dining with at Cipriani's restaurant on Fifth Avenue. The place was noisy and he could hardly hear. In desperation he got up and went outside.

'Father, I can hear you now. Why are you phoning me at two-thirty in the morning your time? Nothing's wrong, is it?'

'I'm afraid it is, Ramon.'

'What? What is wrong?' he asked hoarsely, fear clutching him.

'It is Nena.'

'What's happened to her?' He nearly shouted, pacing the pavement impatiently.

'She's being driven to hospital as we speak. I'm afraid she may lose the baby.'

'The baby? What baby?' he asked, mystified. Then all at once he grasped his father's meaning. 'You mean she's pregnant?' he exclaimed, a new and unprecedented emotion taking hold.

'Yes. Didn't you know?'

'No, I— Is she all right? Oh, what an idiot I've been.'

'Now, calm down, my son. I think you should try and get on the first flight out.'

'Of course. If I leave here immediately I can catch the British Airways flight out of Kennedy,' he said, glancing at his watch, his mind in a frenzy. 'Oh, God, how could this have happened?'

'In the usual way, I imagine,' his father responded dryly. 'Just make sure that in the future you take proper care of your wife. I don't understand all these goings-on between the two of you. It's perfectly ridiculous.'

'Yes, Father. I'll explain when I see you. Please, just make sure she—she and the baby are all right.'

'Very well. I'm on my way to the Chelsea and Westminster Hospital now. Your mother is in the ambulance with Nena. Thank goodness she confided in her, otherwise I dread to think what might have happened.'

Ramon stood on the pavement and gazed blindly at Central Park, at the carriage passing before him with a young couple in the rear, holding hands and hugging, at the lights of the Plaza across the street, seeing nothing but her face, replaying each expression, each moment, each tender look, each instant since that dreadful misunderstanding that had caused so much grief.

Then he took a deep breath and walked back inside the restaurant to explain to his dinner companion what was happening. Without a moment's hesitation Connelly offered to drive him to the airport at once.

Some time later Ramon was dropped at the airport. My goodness, how time passed slowly when you wanted to be somewhere fast, he thought. Why had he made the trip just at this time when it wasn't absolutely essential? Why hadn't he waited? And why had it never occurred to him, when Nena refused that glass of champagne at lunch, that there might be a reason for her refusal?

In the first class departure lounge he quickly dialled his father's mobile phone.

'What's happening?' he asked anxiously. 'Is she all right?'

'We don't know yet. She's with the doctor now, but don't worry—we'll be here with her, never fear.'

'Thank you,' Ramon murmured gratefully, trying to combat the sudden wave of nausea that gripped him at the thought of Nena lying there in the hospital, perhaps losing the baby. Their baby. A baby conceived in one of those torrid moments of—

For a moment Ramon swallowed. He'd never realised it until this very moment, but it was love he felt for Nena. A feeling different from any other he'd ever experienced for any other woman. He shook his head and let out a long sigh, stunned by what he'd just become aware of. He loved her—loved this girl whom he'd known for such a short time, who'd entered his life and taken over in a way that would have been inconceivable to him a very short while ago.

'British Airways flight—' That was his flight.

Grabbing his briefcase, Ramon followed the other passengers and made his way to the plane.

It could not reach London fast enough.

The car was waiting for him at Heathrow to take him to the Chelsea and Westminster Hospital, where he found his mother and father waiting in the corridor outside Nena's room.

'She's been sedated, poor child,' Doña Augusta told him.

'But is she all right? And the baby?' he asked, trying to quell the overwhelming anxiety he'd been suffering all night.

'I'm afraid she's lost it,' his mother answered sadly.

Ramon said nothing, just shoved his hands in his pockets and turned and stared doggedly out of the window. It was his fault all this had occurred. His fault that she'd lived through this horrendous experience alone and unhappy when he should have been next to her. And worse was that it was all because of that dreadful day with Luisa. Had that not occurred, none of this would have happened. It was probably all the anxiety and nervous stress she'd been subjected to that had caused the miscarriage in the first place.

He turned. 'Can I go in and see her?' he asked his mother.

'I think you'd better wait to see the doctor first. He should be here in a few minutes,' his mother demurred.

'Yes,' Don Pedro seconded. 'Wait to speak with the doctor, Ramon. And see to it in the future that you take proper care of your wife,' he added sternly. 'You are not a bachelor any longer, my son. You have duties. Make sure you see to them properly.'

Ramon said nothing, just nodded. His father was right to chastise him. There was no excuse for his absence, only Nena's rejection of him to hang his hat on. But he should have insisted, not allowed her to get the better of him with her arguments. He should have taken charge, as he always did with every other damn aspect of his life, and simply told her how things were going to be—insisted instead of deferring, being gentlemanly and giving way to her wishes. Damn her wishes. He was her husband, after all, and it was his duty and his right to make sure she was properly taken care of.

Several minutes later the doctor put in an appearance.

'Ah! Mr Villalba.'

'Is she all right?' Ramon enquired, features tense.

'Yes. She'll be fine. She's young and in excellent health. But of course a miscarriage is never an easy thing for a woman to go through, no matter how early in the pregnancy it occurs.' He lowered his voice and the two men walked along the corridor. 'She's very upset emotionally. It will require a lot of patience and care on your part to help her through this. Of course the best solution is another baby.'

'Right away?' Ramon looked at him steadily.

'No. Not immediately. She will need a few weeks to get over this, both physically and emotionally.'

Ramon nodded. 'I blame myself for not being here.'

'Don't. These things happen. We don't know why they do, but they do. And it has in no way affected her ability to bear children. Still, once a woman knows she's expecting a baby, has absorbed the fact and has lived even for a few days with the knowledge of another being growing inside her, the sense of loss can be tremendous.'

'I understand.' Ramon nodded. 'May I go in and see her now?'

'Yes. I don't know if she'll be awake yet, but you may stay with her. Don't get into long discussions about all this until she's better, though. There is always a sense of guilt accompanying these things.'

'Thank you, Doctor.' Ramon mustered a smile and shook his hand. 'I'm grateful for all you've done for my wife.'

'I'm afraid I didn't do anything except take care of the problem. The rest will be up to you.' He squeezed Ramon's shoulder, then, after a goodbye and a handshake to Don Pedro and Doña Augusta, he left down the corridor as Ramon prepared to enter Nena's room.

'We'll be leaving now, *querido*. Your father is very tired and must get some rest. If the doctor lets Nena out later today bring her back to Eaton Square. Enough of this being on her own.'

'Of course I will. Go home, Papá, and get some sleep,' Ramon said, touching his father's arm. 'And thank you both for all you've done. I—' There was a catch in his voice.

'It's nothing. We think of her as a daughter,' Doña Augusta said gently. 'See that you mend this breach between you, Ramon, and *don't,*' she begged earnestly, 'let pride and stupidity get in your way, my son.' She reached up and kissed his tense bronzed cheek. 'You will see. God willing, all will be well.'

Ramon quietly opened the door and stared across the bleak hospital room at Nena, lying motionless, like a doll in the centre of the bed. Her hands lay on the white coverlet, and as Ramon approached the bed he reached for one of them, touching it tenderly, a wave of emotion gripping him as he thought of all she'd been through. How scared she must have been, waking up to such a horrible experience in the middle of the night alone, obliged to telephone his parents. And what might have happened if she hadn't phoned? What if she'd been too embarrassed and had stayed there bleeding until morning? What then?

He shuddered and perched on the side of the bed, gazing down at her lovely pale face, her hair lying tidily to each side of it, as though she hadn't stirred. He drew his hand away from hers, afraid of disturbing her, and a rush of tenderness overwhelmed him. She looked like a little girl, lying there so quietly. Yet she was a woman.

His woman.

And in that instant Ramon determined that he would never let her go.

Nena woke to a painful sensation in her lower tummy. Eyes still closed, she winced. Then little by little the events of the previous night shaped themselves in her sedated brain and slowly she opened her eyes.

'Nena, *mia*.'

She heard Ramon's voice, blinked, and stared up at him, her lips parting in an 'oh'. He had come, after all. He was here, had not abandoned her and stayed in New York as she'd feared, but was by her side.

Ramon slipped his hand over hers, then leaned down and softly grazed her lips with his.

'You're here,' she said blurrily.

'Yes, I'm here. And I have no intention of going anywhere.'

Nena registered his words silently, and let him take

her hand in his, feeling the soothing movement of his fingers as he stroked her palm.

'I'm so sorry about the baby,' she said finally, battling a sudden new wave of emotion. 'I shouldn't have—'

'Nena, none of this is your fault.'

'But it is. If I'd—'

'No. I will not permit you to assume any responsibility for this. If anyone is to blame it is I,' he answered bitterly. 'I must have been blind not to recognise that something was different that day in the restaurant. Perhaps you were even going to tell me and it just didn't register.'

'Well, it doesn't matter any more,' she said in a small voice. 'It's too late.'

'Shush. You mustn't get upset. There is time enough to talk of all this once you are better and well again. Now, I am going to see if the doctor will allow you to leave the hospital later today.'

She nodded and closed her eyes, not really caring what happened any more, feeling a great wave of unhappiness for the baby she would never hold in her arms, that tiny piece of life that she'd already pictured alive and kicking, with Ramon's dark eyes and her nose. He—because she was certain it had been a boy—would have looked just like his father...

Silent tears seeped through her tightly closed lids and coursed down her cheeks.

Ramon watched her, helpless. All he could do was wipe the tears away gently with his thumb. There was little else he could do but double his resolve that never again would he allow her to be on her own to suffer.

Later that afternoon Nena was allowed to leave.

She felt tender and fragile, and grateful for Ramon's assistance as together they walked out of the hospital and entered the car. When it pulled up at Eaton Square she looked out of the car window, surprised.

'But I thought I was going home,' she said.

'This is home, Nena.'

'But—'

'No buts,' he said firmly, clasping her hand, and the set of his jaw left her in little doubt of his determination to keep her by him. 'You are staying here with me and that is an end to it.'

'I—' Nena was about to protest, then, too tired to argue, she gave in.

Minutes later she was being taken upstairs and helped into bed by Doña Augusta and one of the maids.

'You need lots of rest, Nena dear. I remember when this happened to me,' Doña Augusta said, sitting on the side of the bed. 'It takes a lot out of you. Emotionally and physically.'

'I hope I'm not being a nuisance,' Nena murmured, the force of habit taking over.

'Rubbish. You are a part of this family now. It is only natural that we should care for you.' She leaned down and dropped a kiss on Nena's forehead. 'Now, try and get some sleep, *querida,* and don't worry— there will be many more babies in the future.'

Nena swallowed the knot in her throat and tried to hold back the tears that were never far from the surface. She nodded.

'No more worrying,' Doña Augusta insisted, patting the coverlet. 'Everything will take care of itself.'

CHAPTER NINE

'How about a trip to Agapos?' Ramon enquired, three weeks later. Nena still seemed very down, lethargic and uninterested in life. Ramon was seriously worried about her. He'd tried to talk about what had happened, but she didn't seem to want to. He'd insisted she see a psychologist, but Nena hadn't derived much benefit from the visits.

'Agapos?' she said, remembering the beautiful island where they'd first made love, where maybe their baby had been conceived.

'Yes. It would do you good to have a break—get away from here and be in the sun. It's lovely in early autumn over there. We would be all by ourselves.'

He reached across and took her hand. Lately she neither accepted or rejected him. It was as though she was living in another world, a place of her own where she didn't allow any intrusions. But Ramon knew—sensed—that either he got through to her emotionally very soon or he might lose her for ever.

'I think we should go down there,' he insisted. 'I shall have the plane ready to take us the day after tomorrow.'

Nena shrugged. She really didn't care what she did any longer. The loss of the baby seemed so tremendous, so incredibly painful. And, although Ramon had been attentive and caring, she just couldn't overcome that little inkling of mistrust that lingered, surfacing every time she was about to let down her guard and let him in.

Would it ever leave her? she wondered. Or would it persist, looming over their marriage, making it impossible for them ever to really come together, for her to trust him fully? After all, what would happen when all this had passed? Say she agreed to live with him and take up a normal life—would she ever be free of the fear of walking into another restaurant and seeing him with another woman? Maybe now he'd be more careful, but she'd learn it from some other source, or simply know instinctively that he was making love to someone else.

Nena sighed. They might as well go to Agapos as be here in London, where it rained all the time and she felt so bleak. Her girlfriends had called, but she had no desire to see them. Or anyone else for that matter. It was as though she'd shored herself up in her own little cocoon, and was loath to leave it in case another nasty surprise caught her off guard.

Ramon, though she didn't know it, had taken heed of the doctor's words and was sleeping in the room next to hers. But as the days went by he was determined that soon they would be sleeping together once again.

Two days later the helicopter was once more hovering over the island, different now in the early autumn light, a soft glow etching the white houses, making them stand out. The blue waters of the Aegean shimmered, the bright coloured fishing boats shining brightly in the lingering sun.

Soon they were up at the house. Nena changed,

donning a comfortable white kaftan, then walked barefoot over the terrace and stared out at the sea, at the late-afternoon sun dipping on the horizon, at more fishing boats returning to port with the day's catch.

It all seemed so peaceful, so distant from London and the mental turmoil of the past weeks. Ramon had been busy the last few days, had seemed to spend a lot of time at the office. She hadn't questioned him about it. Or maybe he was fed up and was beginning another affair with some other woman, she reflected sadly.

Sitting on the balustrade, Nena told herself she must stop being paranoid. It was one thing to realise that the possibility existed, another to assume, with no real reason, that his absence was caused by some new attractive female he'd come across. Still, however hard she tried she was unable to banish that image of Luisa, glancing up at him over her shoulder, of her intimate smile.

Perhaps all the attention Ramon was devoting to her now was just part of his sense of duty, of the obligation he'd undertaken, the promise he'd made to her grandfather. But she didn't want to be considered part of a contractual obligation. She wanted to be wanted for *her*, for who she was.

And that was an unlikely scenario.

At no time had Ramon ever said more than the murmured words spoken in the heat of passion. And those, she realised sadly, meant very little. They were part of a vocabulary he had probably used frequently with every woman he'd bedded.

'Nena?' Ramon stepped out onto the terrace and came to join her on the balustrade. He wore a pair of Bermuda shorts and a T-shirt.

Nena looked at him, surprised. She'd never seen him quite so casual before. And she liked it. She swallowed despite herself at the sight of his strong muscles, still tanned from their previous stay. The overpowering masculine aura still surrounded him, but she'd been less conscious of it over the past few weeks, too tied up with her emotions. Now, as he sat opposite her, his dark hair stirring in the early-evening breeze, his strong arms uncovered, she experienced a charge of desire like nothing she'd felt since before the miscarriage.

She pulled herself up with a jolt.

It was fundamental to remember all the reasons for which a long-term relationship with this man really couldn't work out, all the doubt and the knowledge that he might betray her at any given time. She would have to be firm, she realised with an inner sigh, make a final decision about what she was going to do with her life. It wasn't fair to either of them to linger on in this vacuum of uncertainty.

But it was hard to contemplate life without him at her side. She'd become so used to his presence over the past few weeks—to him popping by in the morning before he left for the office, kissing her tenderly goodbye, ringing her in the late morning to suggest a spontaneous lunch.

It was in the early evening that doubts took hold, when he rang in to say he'd be late because of a meeting or the occasional 'business dinner'. It was then that she asked herself if he was telling her the truth or merely covering tactfully while all the time being ensconced in the arms of some woman or other.

And there was the fact that she hadn't been sleeping with him herself to contend with too.

He was hardly a monk, she recognised, and could hardly be expected to live an entirely celibate life. And if she wasn't sleeping with him, then who was?

It was all so terribly difficult, and Nena gave a deep sigh, wishing things could be different.

'Something wrong, *querida?*' Ramon asked, leaning forward and taking her fingers in his.

The touch of his hand, which for the past few weeks she'd accepted as tenderness and care for her wellbeing, turned suddenly to fire. Nena caught her breath imperceptibly, wanting to draw back, yet staying all the same. Ramon was somehow different here. Not radically. But there was a subtle change. He looked more rugged, more determined, and his eyes held a gleam that she hadn't seen in the past few weeks. She swallowed, felt her body tingle. Was it this place that made her feel so suddenly altered? Was it the gentle breeze blowing in from the sea that was dissipating the pain and unhappiness leaving the way open for the new, unexpected feelings surging through her being?

Ramon drew closer. Night was falling fast, stars peeking in the inky sky. She rose quickly and turned towards the sea, unable to face him.

It had been too long, Ramon decided. He had waited the time she'd needed to recover from the miscarriage, but now he wanted her. Rising, he moved behind her and slipped his hands around her, caressing her ribcage, stopping just below her breast and nuzzling her neck.

Nena gasped, unable to control the rush of desire searing through her like a white-hot arrow. Her breasts ached, and she could feel the soft, moist surrender between her thighs. Then Ramon's thumbs grazed her taut, swollen nipples, very lightly, taunting them through the thin kaftan, slowly, lazily, until she let out a gasp of pleasure. His body pressed against her back, her bottom, and she could feel the full length of him.

Then just as quickly he turned her around and she stood facing him, reading the hunger and determination in his eyes, in the unyielding line of his lips, and knew that he was not going to give in. He would take her. What she wanted was immaterial.

His mouth came down upon hers, and Nena knew a hot rush of exaltation. At first his mouth was tender, as though afraid of hurting her, then all at once she could bear it no longer, knew a raw, primal need for him, could no more control the rampant hunger gnawing at every inch of her body. And as she brought her arms up around his neck and cleaved to him Ramon let drop all barriers, let go the fears he'd had of frightening or hurting her and allowed his mouth to ravage, his tongue to play havoc. He pressed his hand into the small of her back, bringing her closer to him, forcing her to feel the extent of his desire, revelling in her hair, the soft feel of her skin, her scent, her being.

Then, when he could bear it no longer, he did what he'd done once before, and lifting her into his arms carried her masterfully through to the bedroom.

Nena sighed as he laid her on the bed, unable to protest, her whole being pining for him, for his hands on her body, for the feel of him inside her aching core.

And Ramon was quick to satisfy. In one swift movement he lifted her kaftan and threw it aside.

Somehow his own clothes were quickly strewn on the floor and he stood naked.

'My *linda*, my beautiful, lovely Nena,' he murmured hoarsely. 'How I've wanted you, how I've missed you.' Then he was on the bed and his hands were all over her as she writhed, unable to control the spasms of delight overtaking her body as stealthily his fingers ventured within her, easing that delectable yet unbearable pain until she was gorged, filled with the same delicious saturation he'd shown her already, and that, though she hadn't admitted it, she'd missed like the devil.

Ramon crushed his own need, mastered his feelings, delighting in her moans, triumphant when she let go a raw cry of completion when he brought her to a peak.

But this time he didn't wait for her to recover. Instead he thrust deep inside her. For a single instant he experienced a wave of fear that he might be harming her. But Nena's immediate breathless reaction, and her legs curling about him, drove him on and on, dispelling any and all doubt. And once more they travelled as one on an ever-rising journey that ended in a rush of such unadulterated joy that neither could do more than lie gasping, limp in each other's arms.

The next few days were spent in a glorious lazy haze. They spoke little, unwilling to allow anything to obliterate the blissful atmosphere created on their first night, only too ready to let it last for as long as possible. Together they investigated the island in an old army Jeep kept for the purpose. They had picnics up on the rocks overlooking the sea, spent long hours idling away the time, kissing, fondling one another, unable to resist the urgent sexual tug that was present from dawn until dusk.

Nena knew she was deluding herself, that soon she would have to wake up and make up her mind. But for now she didn't care. She was too busy absorbing the whole of Ramon's seductive being—the scent of him, the feel of him, the delicious hours spent trailing her nails over his back, his arms, through his hair. Then suddenly, when she least expected it, he would turn around and with a wolfish grin bring her on top of him, and the whole thing would begin all over again.

Each time they made love he taught her more. Sometimes Nena experienced a stab of shock when they became more experimental, and Ramon positioned her in ways she would never have thought of. But that too excited her, gave her new and exhilarating confidence. She felt truly a woman now, baptised for ever into the art of lovemaking by a man so expert he would be very hard to replace, she realised ruefully, smiling at her own daring.

One day they went out fishing with the villagers. They were friendly and open, and she enjoyed seeing Ramon help heave in the heavy nets. Such a different Ramon, she reflected, from the severe, well-dressed businessman back in London and Buenos Aires. He was getting browner by the day, as she was herself, the soft autumnal sun streaking her hair and seeping into her tanned skin.

Gradually the events of the previous month, the deep sense of loss and fragmentation that she'd experienced faded. She could laugh again, often giggling at Ramon's jokes, amazed at how relaxed he'd become since their arrival on the island. And she was secretly afraid of the day when they would have to leave it. She wished that they could stay on and on, stowed away like luxury castaways, not having to face the ordeals of an everyday life, of the business waiting for him back in London, or the possibility of another woman popping out of the woodwork to destroy the status quo.

In the evenings they sat on the terrace, sipping ouzo or retsina, then sitting down to a late dinner prepared by Efi, the cook, delighting in her melting *moussakas* or delicious *aranaki*—lamb. Occasionally they would take the motor boat and ride over to the nearest island to eat in one of the tavernas by the waterside, where large squid were hung up to dry like washing, then squirted with lemon and cooked on the grill.

Sometimes they would stay there for several hours, and Ramon would play a game or two of backgammon with some of the older villagers, old Petros or Taki, who sat all day, their backs to the warm wall, smoking their strong Turkish tobacco and drinking *cafedaki*—small cups of thick, lethally strong, sweet, black coffee.

When Nena had drunk hers, Maria, the wife of the taverna's owner, would sit down heavily on a creaking wooden chair and turn Nena's cup upside down, allowing the grains to take their course. Then several minutes later—usually after a lengthy conversation with her husband that sounded like a quarrel but that Ramon assured her was not—she would turn back to Nena with a smile and begin telling her fortune, which her grandson of thirteen, Janis, translated into surprisingly fluent English.

'She says you are married to a good man but you don't trust him,' he said one day, as his grandmother placed the cup back in the saucer and looked at her understandingly. 'She says it is normal. Kirios Ramon is a very handsome man. His cup says he had many women. But not any more.'

'Right. Well, thanks,' Nena said hastily, looking up uneasily, hoping his words had been drowned by the lapping of the water and the *sirtaki* music playing on the radio, and that Ramon, seated two tables away, hadn't heard.

'Want a game, Nena?' he called. 'I've just been beaten by Petros. He's the best player on the island. But we still have time for one more before we get back.'

Then he glanced out to sea and said something to Petros in Greek. The old man narrowed his eyes and peered across the water.

'Actually, I think we'd better go after all. Petros says there may well be a storm brewing. It's autumn now, and these things can whip up out of the blue at this time of year. I'll play you at home, *mi linda,* how's that?'

Nena could think of other games to play at home, but she agreed, picked up her basket and the straw hat that had become a part of her island uniform and, saying goodbye to the islanders, moved with Ramon towards the motor boat.

They were three-quarters of the way back when the storm struck. The sky turned purple and dark, heavy black clouds loomed, lightning flashed and the wind picked up. Huge waves heaved to and fro, making it difficult to steer the small motor boat.

'Hang on tight,' Ramon said, ploughing mercilessly

through the rising waters. 'We'll be there soon. Are you okay?' He sent her a worried glance, then concentrated once more on steering.

'I'm fine,' Nena shouted, disguising her fear.

Then all at once an immense wave rocked the boat off balance, nearly sweeping them into the deep.

'Hold on!' Ramon shouted, as they clung, drenched, to the boat. 'Grab a life jacket.'

Nena did as she was told, and with difficulty pulled on the floatable life jacket. Ramon was just doing the same when a clap of thunder sounded and another huge wave rammed into them. Before Ramon could do anything they capsized.

Nena felt her body catapulted into the deep waters of the Aegean. Where was Ramon? Oh, God. She spluttered and tried desperately to hold on to the boat, that was still near enough to clutch.

'Ramon!' she shouted desperately as soon as she surfaced. 'Ramon, where are you? Answer me.' She could just distinguish Agapos and realised that they were not far from land. But would somebody see them? Would anybody be out in this weather and able to rescue them? And where was Ramon? Why didn't he reply?

A horrible vice-like fear gripped her as she tried desperately to fight her way around the capsized craft to see if she could find him. Maybe he'd been knocked out in the fall. Maybe— *Oh, God, no— please, dear God, make him be safe, make him be alive.*

She was finding it hard to stay afloat as the waves rushed at her, sweeping her and the boat in their wake. She could hardly breathe as water filled her lungs and she went under once more, before spluttering back to the surface, desperate to find him.

Then suddenly she heard the distant rumble of a motor and a wave of relief poured over her. Someone had sighted them. Thank goodness. If only she could reach Ramon.

But what if he'd been swept away and—? No—she mustn't think like that. He was here, close by, she was certain. He just couldn't call to her.

Then at last she saw men from the island leaning over the side of a small, sturdy fishing boat, undaunted by the turbulent sea. They came up close, then one threw her a cord with a lifesaver attached and urged her to hold on to it as he pulled her in.

Shivering, she climbed on board, oblivious of her cuts and bruises, her eyes searching the water for any sign of the man she loved.

She loved!

Suddenly the words sprang at her. How hadn't she recognised it fully before? Why had she not admitted to herself just how much he actually meant to her?

Then she heard a shout and watched frozen to the spot as one of the men, wearing a life jacket and secured by a rope, jumped in and swam towards an inert form floating nearby.

Nena gripped the side of the boat and gazed in terror as the man slipped his hand under Ramon's chin and brought him in the lifesaving position back to the fishing boat. There were shouts and exclamations as the men heaved him on board and Tasso began immediately to pump his lungs.

Nena stood by, terrified, fearing to interfere lest she get in the way. *Come on,* she begged silently. *Please, dear God, make him all right. Please don't let him die.*

After some thirty seconds she heard a cough, and watched, trembling, as Ramon spluttered and wretched.

'Oh, darling,' she cried, throwing herself on the deck and reaching for him.

Ramon spluttered again, and gulped, and tried to open his eyes. He'd been hit hard on the head and was reeling from the shock and pain.

'Breathe deeply, darling,' Nena urged as the boat turned and ploughed steadily back towards Agapos and safety.

She held him in her arms, feeling him limp on her breast as he lay there, too exhausted to move, to do anything but try and breathe. Soon they were docking in the tiny harbour at Agapos, and men rushed aboard and lifted Ramon easily in their arms.

Nena followed close behind as they carried him into the nearest villager's home and laid him on a simple wooden bed, above which hung a large Greek cross and a picture of Hagios Stefanos—St Stephen— the patron saint of the area.

Women came in and began treating him. The owner of the house was named Elpida. Luckily her son, who was a doctor in Athens, was visiting for the weekend, and came hurrying in with his medical bag. He pulled out his stethoscope and carefully began listening to Ramon's heaving lungs while Nena stood by in agony, waiting for the verdict, wishing she could wave a magic wand and make him all right.

Slowly Ramon's breathing became easier. The doctor went about his business, and little by little he began to register what was going on around him.

'Nena?' he whispered hoarsely, his voice a thread. 'Where is she? Is she all right?'

'I'm here, darling, and I'm fine.' She sat down next to him on the bed and smoothed his brow, wincing at the sight of the cut on his cheek where the boat must have hit him. 'Darling, you're fine. Everything's all right now. You're going to be all right.'

Ramon's eyes met hers for a moment and he tried to smile. 'I thought I'd lost you,' he whispered, the words obviously an effort.

'Don't talk, darling, just stay quiet,' Nena admonished, her fingers entwining his, watching as his head sank back on the pillow.

The doctor reassured her, 'He'll be much better in a few hours, once he's had some rest.'

'But I thought people who'd had concussion should stay awake,' Nena countered, looking at him uncertainly.

'Don't worry,' the doctor replied in excellent English, 'We'll keep an eye on him. Now, I recommend that you let me take a look at you. A few cuts and bruises as well, I see.'

Nena looked down at her arms and legs. It was true. There were a couple of bruises forming on her arm, and a cut just above her knee.

'Let me treat them,' the doctor said firmly, seeing how loath she was to leave Ramon's side even for a minute. 'Your husband will be fine now. All he needs is some rest.'

Reluctantly Nena rose and allowed him to disinfect her cut and put a bandage round it. But she never took her eyes off Ramon's sleeping figure.

They stayed there all night—Ramon sleeping peacefully in the little wooden bed, with Nena seated on a stool next to him, never taking her eyes off him, gently smoothing the hair from his brow from time to time. As dawn broke she saw how pale he was and her heart lurched once more with fear. Was he really all right? He had to be. She couldn't bear it if he wasn't.

There was no sign of yesterday's storm now. The day dawned bright and sunny, and soon the household was up and moving. Nena could hear Elpida's movements in the kitchen, could smell the scent of fresh coffee and baked bread and hear the low murmuring of voices.

Then Elpida peeked around the door.

'Ti kani?' she asked.

'Better, I think,' Nena answered in English, smiling.

'Eisai kourasmeni,' Elpida said, and Nena understood enough to realise she was telling her she must be tired.

Only then did she become aware of the stiffness in her limbs, and a mild throbbing in her leg. Elpida was indicating to her that she must go and rest. But first she gave Nena a cup of steaming coffee, which she drank thankfully. She had refused all food the night before, unable to stomach anything. But now, seeing Ramon pale but better, and certain that he was on the road to recovery, she relaxed a little and realised that she was in fact quite hungry.

Elpida pointed to the kitchen and insisted she join the family for a breakfast of thick hunks of bread spread with home-made butter and fresh honey. It tasted glorious, and as she bit into it Nena sent up thanks for their timely delivery from what could have been a fatal accident.

Then she returned to Ramon's bedside, watching

him tenderly, hoping that soon he would open those wonderful chestnut eyes and smile at her as only he knew how.

'I can't believe we've been here three weeks,' Nena said one evening as they sat with jerseys slipped over their shoulders, for the nights were much cooler now. Ramon had made a surprisingly quick recovery but he still needed to rest.

'It has passed so quickly,' Ramon agreed, slipping his hand in hers and squeezing her fingers. 'Thank you, *mi amor,* for caring for me as you have. I couldn't ask for a better wife.' He grinned at her, the cut on his cheek practically healed now and the bruises barely visible.

'You aren't an altogether easy patient,' she chided, recalling the first few days after the accident, when Ramon had begun to recuperate, demanding to get up, impatient at being kept quiet when he wanted to be active. But Nena had insisted, and for some reason he could not put his finger on, Ramon had complied with her wishes.

'Another glass of wine?' he asked, leaning the bottle in the direction of her glass while glancing at his watch. 'I have a couple of calls to make in about twenty minutes—just time to sit here a little longer.'

'Okay.' Nena smiled. She loved these evenings spent on the terrace, sharing time together—moments that had become increasingly precious after the accident.

The latter had formed a silent bond between them. They didn't need to talk about it, or go over it time and again, but each knew how close they'd been to losing the other and the thought had left them both shaken.

'Ah, there's the phone,' Ramon remarked, getting up from the wrought-iron chair and making his way inside.

Nena caught snatches of his voice through the open glass doors.

'Yes? When did you find out? Ah, I see. Well, it will have to be dealt with immediately. I was sure he was the one. I'm afraid so—no, that would be impossible. Fine. I'll be there tomorrow.'

Nena listened to his last words with a sinking heart. She knew the call must be from London, that something was going on in the office—either his or at Carvajal's—that would require his immediate presence. Now, finally, the dream was about to end.

'Nena, I'm afraid we shall have to leave tomorrow and go back to London. There are things I need to attend to at the office,' he said absently.

'I see,' she replied, masking the rush of fear and disappointment. Here everything was so perfect that she was loath to return to the real world. 'Is something wrong?' she asked, seeing his brows creased in a thick dark line above the ridge of his nose.

'I'm not entirely certain as yet, but I believe so. It's a bit difficult to explain right now.'

'Well, I don't see why,' Nena responded touchily. 'I'm not totally dense.'

'It has nothing to do with you being dense or otherwise. I'm just not sure of my facts and this involves others. I'm afraid you'll have to wait.' His tone was arbitrary and she experienced a flash of annoyance.

And pain.

It had already begun. The outside world was al-

ready insinuating itself into their little paradise, taint-
ing it with the doubts and fears that for the past weeks
she'd managed to exclude from their existence.

And now was reality check.

Nena said nothing, but she rose and went inside,
all desire to sit out in the evening breeze suddenly
gone. The magic interlude was over, she realised
sadly, and the sooner she recognised the fact the better it would be.

CHAPTER TEN

Since their return home Nena had barely seen Ramon. He seemed inordinately busy, often returning to Eaton Square close upon ten o'clock. She didn't question his absences, but they hurt. Surely there couldn't be *that* much to do at the office that required him to stay so late? One night she actually telephoned him on his mobile phone, but she was given short shrift and never repeated the action.

'I'm in a meeting,' he'd said impatiently. 'I'll call you as soon as I've finished.'

But it was past midnight when he reached home, and Nena had long since cried herself to sleep.

It was no use. It would always be the same. The few weeks away had been nothing but an illusion that they'd both bought into for a while. Now he was back in his own world—a world of business and possibly casual or less casual affairs—and all that went with it.

The other thing that worried her was that they'd hardly made love since their return. This fact, coupled with the late nights and Ramon's increasingly short temper, did nothing to allay her fears.

She must, she realised, make up her mind whether or not she was going to continue with the marriage or bring it to an end once and for all.

The other matter that she'd left on hold was the

applications to the universities she was interested in. But for some reason she didn't have the energy or the will to get on with them. Perhaps she would just have to let it go for another year.

Life was altogether not bright, and Nena felt herself slowly withering.

There seemed little light at the end of the tunnel.

As his investigation deepened Ramon became increasingly angry at the discrepancies he was coming across—not only in the Carvajal accounting, but in the way several big deals had been handled. It was a gruelling job to try and get to the bottom of the whole thing without alerting the principal suspects, and it had to be done carefully, mostly out of hours. He had enough to keep him busy during the day anyway, running not only his own businesses but seeing that Don Rodrigo's affairs were put back on track.

His days were long and his nights short. He wished he could explain to Nena, but felt it was impossible—the whole thing was just too tricky and too delicate to be broadcast before he had definite answers and proof of the double-dealing he suspected.

But when one weekend he suggested they go to Paris and take a break she seemed unenthusiastic. She didn't want to open up her grandfather's flat there, and said they might as well just go to a hotel.

Ramon agreed, and booked a suite at the Plaza Athénée.

They arrived in Paris on Friday evening and prepared to dine at the Relais Plaza attached to the hotel. Perhaps later they would go dancing or have a drink somewhere, he reflected as they sat down.

But Nena was strangely silent, unwilling even to make conversation.

'Nena, is something wrong?' he asked, irritated despite his desire to spend a nice time with her. She certainly wasn't making it easy. Hadn't he been at her entire disposal during three full weeks? Surely she must understand that he had a lot of work to catch up with now, as well as his other responsibilities?

'No, nothing's wrong—except everything,' she muttered, savagely spreading butter on her French roll.

'What do you mean, *querida?* I thought we were past all that now, that things were settling down between us.'

'Really?' she said, glaring at him across the table. 'Well, you thought wrong. Maybe you think you can just shove me into a convenient drawer the minute you have other priorities to deal with, but I think that I merit some consideration.'

Ramon sighed. This was not going to be easy. The investigations had reached a critical point where any kind of revelation might be fatal to the final outcome.

'Look, Nena, I know I've been out a lot—'

'A lot? Talk about an understatement?'

'Please,' he pleaded patiently, 'I can't explain everything that goes on at the office to you, but right now there are some fires to be put out.'

'I'm sure. Especially from six o'clock onwards.'

'Nena, what exactly are you saying?'

'That you seem to have an awful lot to do after hours, Ramon.'

He looked at her haughtily. 'As a matter of fact, I do.'

'Great. Well, that tells me all I need to know, doesn't it?'

'What are you implying?' he asked carefully, lowering his glass, his eyes narrowing dangerously and his mouth forming a thin, angry line.

'That you obviously have a mistress. Which is why I think the best thing would be if we finally brought this whole rigmarole to an end.'

'You want to end our marriage?' he said bitingly.

'Yes. I think that this time I've really reached the end of my tether, Ramon. First it was Luisa, and now— Well, I don't know who it is now, but I can only deduce there must be someone for you to spend every night out with as you're doing.' Her eyes were bright, her smile fixed and brittle, but she kept it in place, damned if she was going to make a fool of herself again.

'This is absurd,' he threw, putting his napkin down on the table angrily.

'No, it's not. You think that you can handle me as if I was a piece of personal property that you can pick up or put back on the shelf whenever you feel like it. Well, I'm not. And the sooner you realise it the better. The problem is that I don't think you're capable of seeing it any other way, so the sooner we get divorced and get on with our respective lives, the better it will be for both of us.'

'I don't believe I'm hearing this,' he muttered, hot rage simmering below his cool exterior.

'Don't you? Well, that's because you're too used to getting your own way, I suppose.' Nena made a show of sipping her champagne.

'Okay, that's it.' Ramon's face was dark and forbidding now and Nena swallowed, wondering if she'd gone too far. But it served him right. He had no right to treat her the way he had, in that autocratic manner.

'Waiter.' Ramon signalled the young man. 'We won't be dining after all. Put it on my bill.' He made to rise.

'But we've just ordered!' Nena exclaimed.

'Get up, Nena, and come with me.'

Nena hesitated, about to refuse, then realised that she could hardly make a scene in the middle of the Relais and obediently followed him.

Ramon marched her out of the restaurant and down the corridor back into the hotel. There he called the elevator. They rode it in chilled silence that could be cut with a knife. Nena held her head high and pretended not to give a damn, but she couldn't help peeking at his furious face. What did he plan to do? Pack up and leave for London again at once?

Ramon unlocked the door of their suite and pulled off the jacket of his suit. Then he turned and eyed her, his eyes hard. 'I've had just about enough of these games.'

'What games? I'm not playing games. If anyone does that it's you,' she threw, standing her ground.

'Really? You think I play games? That I spend the better part of my time with some woman instead of with you, is that it?' he asked, voice menacing.

Nena took a deep breath determined not to cower as he moved towards her.

'I—yes. I think that—'

'What exactly do you think, Nena? Tell me,' he said, looming over her now, his dark eyes gleaming with anger.

'That you're—well, that—'

'Yes? Say it. Go on—or are you afraid?'

'Of course I'm not afraid,' she spluttered, forcing herself to look him in the eye. 'It's just that—'

'What?'

'This whole thing was wrong right from the start,' she muttered, looking away.

'Really? Well, let me show you just how wrong I think it is.'

Before she could react his arms were about her, his body ramming hers. His hand slipped to the crook of her neck and he pulled her hair back, forcing her to look into his face. 'I'll show you once and for all what is right and what is wrong, *señora mia,*' he muttered hoarsely, practically throwing her onto the bed.

Then he was kissing her, stripping her of her garments and laying her naked before him.

'Don't, Ramon,' she whispered, feeling that inevitable tug of desire pulling somewhere deep within her and trying desperately to resist it. 'Don't, please—we must be reasonable.'

'Reasonable? Ha!' With a few quick movements he stripped off his clothes and was back on the bed, his mouth ravaging her breasts, causing her to cry out. Then his lips sought further, descending until they reached her most vulnerable spot, that tiny nub of flesh, which he laved, taunted, leaving her moaning, the indescribable pleasure more intense than anything she'd ever felt, even in their most ardent lovemaking on Agapos.

And he didn't stop, but continued relentlessly until she climaxed over and over, unable to prevent the thrilling rush of pleasure and fulfilment.

Nena could do nothing to stop the ardent onslaught, all thoughts forgotten as her plundered being surrendered to Ramon's merciless siege of her body. When finally he thrust inside her, not gently, but hard and fast, as though determined to possess every inch of her, she curled around him, basked in the delight of him, breathless, responding now kiss for kiss, arching to receive him, all reason forgotten.

When it was over at last, and they lay spent among the rumpled linen sheets, Ramon on one side of the bed and Nena on the other, he turned and looked at her hard. 'Is that what you call wrong, Nena? Would you be able to conceive doing that with another man?'

'Of course I wouldn't dream of making love with another man,' she threw at him witheringly, wishing he would take her in his arms as he usually did, not leave her abandoned and alone on the far side of this very large bed.

'I see. And you think that I would find it perfectly natural to make love in the same manner as I do with you with another woman? Is that it?'

'It had occurred to me,' she mumbled, feeling rather foolish under his intense scrutiny. 'After all, you were out with Luisa.'

'Luisa! Always damn Luisa. Can't we forget her? I certainly have. She's nothing but a friend now.'

'That's not what it looked like to me,' Nena muttered, curling into the pillow, her tired limbs aching.

'So you're jealous?' he said thoughtfully, sitting up and eyeing her closely.

'Of course I'm not jealous,' she snapped, sitting up as well and pulling her knees under her chin. 'I'm realistic, that's all. You had an affair with the woman for two years. I suppose it's normal that you wouldn't just break up with her because of a marriage of convenience that was thrust upon you when you least expected it.'

'Hmm.' His gaze was speculative. 'And just out of interest, *querida,* how did you find out about Luisa and I?'

'I read an article,' she replied defensively. 'In *Hola!* magazine. You were splattered all over it.'

'I see. And so you believe that now I must be either continuing my affair with Luisa—an interesting thought, since she's several thousand miles away—or out every evening making passionate love to someone else?'

'I didn't say that.'

'Not in so many words,' he said, his lips twitching, 'but you implied it.'

'Well, you have to admit you spend more time out than in,' she threw, eyeing him crossly from under her thick lashes, unaware of how lovely and young and vulnerable she looked, huddled against the pillows, her lips pouting.

'Then perhaps it is time, *mi amor,* that I explain to you exactly why I have been spending an unusual amount of time away from you. It is not by desire, I assure you.'

'No? Then why is it?' she challenged, wondering what sort of excuse he'd come up with—though she was feeling less certain about her former theory by the moment.

'Perhaps we should get up first, have a shower, and I'll order Room Service,' Ramon replied, reaching over and helping her up. 'Then I promise to give you a full account of why I've been so tied up.'

'But—'

'Shush,' he ordered. 'For once just do as you're told, and don't get me annoyed again or this time I'll lay you over my knee and give you the spanking you deserve for being so suspicious of your husband,' he said, laughing before he leaned down and kissed her brow. 'Now, off with you into the shower.'

He slapped her bottom lightly, and Nena felt her face breaking into a smile in spite of the doubts that still lingered.

Later, once they'd both showered, Nena joined Ramon at the table brought up by Room Service, piled with scrambled eggs and bacon, toast and tea. They sat wrapped in the thick terry towel robes provided by the hotel and Nena realised that she was hungry now—and for just what he'd ordered. Forget wine and fine cuisine, she was delighted to dig her teeth into something wholesome.

'I hope this suits you,' Ramon said, passing the butter. 'Personally, I'm rather hungry.'

'Me, too,' Nena agreed, lifting the silver dome covering her scrambled eggs and bacon and delighting in the delicious aroma wafting to her nostrils.

This she realised wistfully, was another aspect of her husband that she so enjoyed. The fact that he could be fun, casual and relaxed. That she didn't need to be on show the whole time, like some wives appeared to be, that she could be herself.

But she still hadn't heard what he had to say, and she was determined that before she allowed herself any more breaks she simply must know what Ramon had been doing for the past few weeks. Even though she had her own ideas, the least she could do was listen to his version of the story before passing final judgement.

She looked across the crisp white tablecloth at his

handsome features, his bronzed face and neck appearing from inside the white terry robe, and sighed.

How she loved him!

Nena took some toast from the basket and absently spread it with butter. For, although she recognised her feelings, she knew that unless his excuse was a very good one she could never live happily with a man whom she believed was betraying her at every turn—however handsome, however wonderful he might be.

'Are—are you going to tell me?' she said finally, biting the bullet. Better to get it over with right away than spend the whole meal conjecturing.

'I told you I would tell you, Nena, and I will. It may come as a surprise, and be somewhat upsetting, but I'm afraid it's the truth and must be faced.'

Nena nodded. Her heart quailed. So it was a woman after all.

'Ever since your grandfather died,' Ramon said, stirring some sugar into his tea, 'I have been dealing with the Carvajal affairs, as you know.'

She nodded, gulped down her tea and listened.

'After several days of studying files, and meeting with members of the board and the staff, I became aware of certain discrepancies. Or what I assumed might be discrepancies. One file in particular caught my attention. I won't bore you with a lot of detail that is really unimportant at this stage—suffice it to say that I became increasingly suspicious of several people, and principally, I'm sorry to say, Sir Wilfred.'

'Sir Wilfred?' Nena exclaimed, shocked. 'But he was Grandfather's most trusted person.'

'I know. Which makes what I've discovered doubly bad.'

'What have you discovered?' Nena asked, caught

between shock at his revelation and delight that the reason he'd been spending time away was so far removed from what her fertile imagination had been creating that it left her feeling stupid and guilty for having falsely accused Ramon.

'I'm afraid he's been siphoning funds from the company ever since your grandfather became ill. But it'll be difficult to prove, and I would hesitate to take the matter to court. It will only cause a scandal, and would probably affect the market value of the company as a whole. I feel we should deal with this as discreetly as possible. Sir Wilfred is, after all, getting on. It would be no surprise to anyone if he decided to retire.'

'But that's awful!' Nena exclaimed, horrified that such a trusted member of her grandfather's entourage could have stooped to this level. 'How could he have done this to Grandfather when he knew how much he was trusted? It's awful, Ramon. He shouldn't get away with it.'

He shrugged. 'I know he shouldn't, but believe me, Nena, this is the best way to deal with the matter. It'll avoid an uproar, and the company has not suffered very much from his devious behaviour. Mercifully, he hasn't had time to do much damage.'

'No—thanks to you,' she said, her eyes meeting his across the table.

'I did nothing but my duty. This sort of thing is precisely why your grandfather wanted someone responsible at the helm. I was merely doing my job.'

Nena smiled tentatively. 'Perhaps that's true, but— well, I feel awful that I imagined so many things about you.'

'You aren't entirely to blame,' he responded ruefully, reaching for her hand and stroking her fingers. 'I did nothing to alleviate those doubts. I couldn't, you see. I didn't want to upset you unnecessarily, and I didn't feel I could voice my opinion until I had absolute proof of what Sir Wilfred was doing.'

'I understand. How stupid I've been.'

'Not at all. I rather like that my wife is jealous of me. I would be just the same about you.'

'Would you?' she asked, colouring, suddenly curious.

'Yes. Don't even think about having any good-looking young men hanging around.'

'I wouldn't dream of it,' Nena said, smiling at him. 'I'm quite happy with what I've got.'

'Are you? I certainly hope so. Because I am. More than happy.' He rose, came around the table and, slipping his hands around her neck from behind, firmly kissed the top of her head.

'You're sure this marriage isn't just an obligation for you?' she queried once again, needing to be certain, to feel absolutely sure before she committed.

'Tell me, what does it look like to you, *mi amor?* Do I seem bored to you? Unhappy? Not forthcoming in bed?'

'No, of course not.'

'Then what are you worried about?'

'I don't know. Nothing any more, I suppose. It just seemed so—so imposed, so businesslike.'

'Let's face the truth of the matter, Nena. My parents and your grandfather were right. Despite this being a totally intolerable situation by today's standards they've proved us wrong.' He pulled her up and they faced one another. 'Frankly, all I want to do is take you back into bed and see if together we can't make another baby as soon as possible.'

'Oh.' Nena stared at his chest and swallowed, the thought of the baby sending a shaft of pain searing through her.

'Nena, the miscarriage happened because the time wasn't right. We weren't completely sure of one another, and somehow nature understood that and took care of things in its own fashion. But not any more. This time I will be here, next to you, making sure nothing happens to you ever again.'

'And Luisa?' she asked in a small voice, needing to cover every piece of terrain.

'I explained to her that day at the restaurant. That's why I met with her. To tell her once and for all that it was over between us, that I had found the woman of my dreams and that there was no possibility of us having any kind of relationship except friendship.'

'Really?' Nena raised her face to his, a rush of relief and warmth coursing through her at the gleam in his bright chestnut eyes, at the possessive look he sent her and the delicious feel of his hands caressing her back.

'Let's get one thing clear, Nena,' he said, drawing away from her and posing his hands on her shoulders. 'I will never lie to you. Either you trust me and I trust you or this relationship makes no sense. Do you trust me?'

She looked at him for a long moment, drinking in his words. Then she smiled, looked straight into his eyes.

'Yes, I do.'

'For as long as we live?'

'Until death do us part,' she whispered in response.

'Then there's very little left to say,' he murmured, drawing her close, 'that can't be said in other ways.'

Scooping her into his arms as though she were a feather, he held her a moment, gazing into her eyes. 'You are mine,' he declared, 'all mine. And I shall never, ever let you go.'

'Ditto,' she murmured, letting her head sink onto his strong shoulder.

Ramon took her to the bed and laid her in the middle of it. 'Now, it's time to get down to augmenting our small family, *señora mia*,' he said, a wolfish grin spreading over his features.

'And I'll be only too happy to oblige, kind sir,' she whispered, pulling him down onto the bed, where he landed on top of her.

'Then let's get to it.'

'Wait—hadn't we better put the ''do not disturb'' sign out?' Nena asked suddenly.

'Forget it,' he growled. 'They'll get the message soon enough when there's no answer. Now, can we please forget about anything that isn't just us, Nena?'

'Anything you say, my love,' she replied demurely, smothering the gurgle of love and laughter bubbling inside. 'Anything you say.'

*   *   *   *   *

If you have enjoyed
THE SOCIETY BRIDE,
you might like to know that

Fiona Hood-Stewart

*is also one of the
International Collection
of bestselling authors
writing for MIRA Books.
Next month (May 2004)
sees the publication of her
newest novel,*

SOUTHERN BELLE.

*Here is a delicious extract
to tempt you…*

CHAPTER ONE

LEANING on his ski poles at the bottom of the slope, Johnny Graney watched appreciatively as the slim white-clad figure crossed the last few hundred yards, then made a neat, sharp stop next to him.

"Okay?" he enquired solicitously.

"Fine." Elm pressed the tip of her pole into the back of her binding.

Johnny followed suit, wishing she'd remove her glasses once more so he could catch another glimpse of those incredible brown eyes, an amazing contrast to the mass of natural blonde hair falling about her shoulders.

As though guessing his silent wish, Elm shook her skis, then removed her glasses. For a moment he frowned. He knew that face. Was she an actress? Someone he'd met in London?

"How about a hot chocolate in the village?" he threw casually, surprising himself.

"Oh, I really don't think—"

"You said you were sorry for running into me." He grinned, his blue eyes flashing in his bronzed face. "Make up for it by joining me."

Elm was about to refuse automatically when she suddenly realized she wouldn't mind having a drink with this handsome stranger. It was Gstaad, after all, not Chicago. Everybody knew each other.

"Okay, why not?" She smiled.

"Great. Maybe we should introduce ourselves. In a formal manner," he added, lips twitching.

Elm grinned ruefully.

"You first," he urged in a smooth British accent.

"Elm Hathaway from Savannah, Georgia."

"Pleased to meet you, Elm Hathaway from Savannah, Georgia. I'm Johnny Graney from Ireland."

A warm tingle coursed through Elm's fingers. Then all at once realization dawned.

"Johnny Graney?"

"Guilty." He sent her a curious glance. "This sounds like a line, but haven't we met before?"

"Uh, as a matter of fact, we have," Elm responded, feeling as if she'd been thrown into a time warp. Johnny Graney had been her first serious crush, the boy she'd mooned over some twenty years earlier.

"I'm dreadfully sorry, but I—" He raised his hands in a gesture of defeat. "I'm afraid I just don't remember."

"How flattering," Elm replied dryly. "But it makes sense. At the time, you were only peripherally aware of my existence."

"I was?" His face took on a look of comical horror. "You must be joking," he added. "If I'd ever met you, even for a split second, I'm certain I'd remember."

Elm burst out laughing. He'd been a dangerous flirt back then, and every girl's hero. She couldn't resist teasing him a little longer. "I can see I made a lasting impression on you," she said, glancing down.

"Look, I feel awful. At least give me a hint," he begged.

"Should I?" she taunted, deliciously aware that she was actually flirting with a man, something she hadn't done in years.

"Come on, be a sport. Heck, you almost massacred me back there. Are you planning torture, too?" He raised an amused brow, and Elm smiled sweetly.

"It's too cold for conversation."

"Okay. The Palace Hotel—I promise a table next to the fireplace if you tell me where we met."

"That's blackmail."

"Elm Hathaway from Savannah, Georgia," he said thoughtfully, placing their skis on the back of a new silver Range Rover.

"This is really quite demoralizing." She pouted, sighing heavily as he held the door of the vehicle for her. "To think I've changed to the point of being unrecognizable—"

"I never said that, I merely—"

"I know," she continued, enjoying the game. "You meet so many women it's hard to keep track. Don't worry, I understand." She sent him a sympathetic look.

"Hey! Hold it," he exclaimed. "If it was as long ago as you're implying, maybe you were an ugly duckling who's since turned into a swan."

"An ugly duckling—" Elm spluttered, laughing. "I was never an ugly duckling."

"In that case you'll just have to help me out," he insisted.

"I don't know." She eyed him thoughtfully. "Seeing you strain your memory is rather satisfying."

"I give up," Johnny declared dramatically.

"What—so easily?" She raised a brow and looked him over with a contemptuous grin. "I seem to recall

a certain basketball team captain rallying his players
with a speech about never giving up and fighting until
the death... Quite dramatic stuff, really,'' she added
with a sigh, "and so disappointing to know it no
longer holds true."

The car braked abruptly. "My God." He turned
and stared at her. "Now I remember. Little Elm
Hathaway, the Southern Belle from Savannah."

The world's bestselling romance series.

HARLEQUIN®
Presents

Seduction and Passion Guaranteed!

OUTBACK KNIGHTS
Marriage is their mission!

From bad boys—to powerful,
passionate protectors!

Three tycoons from the Outback
rescue their brides-to-be....

**Coming soon in Harlequin Presents:
Emma Darcy's exciting new trilogy**

Meet Ric, Mitch and Johnny—once three Outback bad
boys, now rich and powerful men. But these sexy city
tycoons must return to the Outback to face a new
challenge: claiming their women as their brides!

**MAY 2004: THE OUTBACK MARRIAGE RANSOM #2391
JULY 2004: THE OUTBACK WEDDING TAKEOVER #2403
NOVEMBER 2004: THE OUTBACK BRIDAL RESCUE #2427**

*"Emma Darcy delivers a spicy love story...
a fiery conflict and a hot sensuality."
—Romantic Times*

Available wherever Harlequin books are sold.

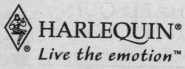

HARLEQUIN®
Live the emotion™

Visit us at www.eHarlequin.com

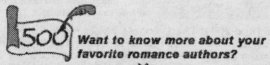

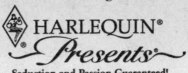

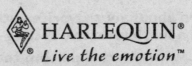

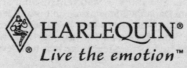

Coming Next Month

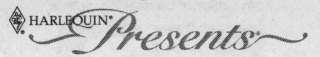

HARLEQUIN *Presents*

THE BEST HAS JUST GOTTEN BETTER!

#2391 THE OUTBACK MARRIAGE RANSOM Emma Darcy
At sixteen, Ric Donato wanted Lara Seymour—but they were worlds apart. Years later he's a city tycoon, and now he can have anything he wants.... Lara is living a glamorous life with another man, but Ric is determined to have her—and he'll do whatever it takes....

#2392 THE STEPHANIDES PREGNANCY Lynne Graham
Cristos Stephanides wanted Betsy Mitchell the moment he saw her, shy and prim in her chauffeur's outfit, at the wheel of his limousine.... However, the Greek tycoon hadn't bargained on being kidnapped—along with Betsy—and held captive on an Aegean island!

#2393 A SICILIAN HUSBAND Kate Walker
When Terrie Hayden met Gio Cardella she knew that there was something between them. Something that was worth risking everything for. But the proud Sicilian didn't want to take that risk. He had no idea what force kept dragging him back to her door....

#2394 THE DESERVING MISTRESS Carole Mortimer
May Calendar has spent her life looking after her sisters and running the family business—and she's determined not to let anyone take it away from her! Especially not arrogant tycoon Jude Marshall! But sexy, charming Jude is out to wine and dine her—how can she resist...?

**#2395 THE MILLIONAIRE'S MARRIAGE DEMAND
Sandra Field**
Julie Renshaw is shocked when Travis Strathern makes an outrageous demand: marriage! She is very attracted to him—but is she ready to marry for convenience? Travis always gets his own way—but Julie makes it clear that their marriage must be based on love as well as passion....

#2396 THE DESERT PRINCE'S MISTRESS Sharon Kendrick
Multimillionaire Darian Wildman made an instant decision about beautiful Lara Black—he had to have her! Their mutual attraction was scorching! Then Darian made a discovery that would change both their lives. He was the illegitimate heir to a desert kingdom—and a prince!